Idle Ingredients

ALSO BY MATT WALLACE

IDLE
INGREDIENTS

MATT WALLACE

A TOM DOHERTY ASSOCIATES BOOK

NEW YORK

This is a work of fiction. All of the characters, organizations, and events portrayed in this novella are either products of the author's imagination or are used fictitiously.

IDLE INGREDIENTS

Copyright © 2017 by Matt Wallace

Cover photograph © Getty Images
Cover design by Peter Lutjen

Edited by Lee Harris

A Tor.com Book
Published by Tom Doherty Associates
175 Fifth Avenue
New York, NY 10010

www.tor.com

Tor® is a registered trademark of
Macmillan Publishing Group, LLC.

ISBN 978-0-7653-9002-8 (ebook)
ISBN 978-0-7653-9003-5 (trade paperback)

First Edition: February 2017

PART I

NEW REGIME

SHORT ORDER

By her sixth egg of the morning the water in Lena's poaching pan is a cloudy mess, but the breakfast rush affords her no time to change it out with new water and bring that to heat.

Her concentration is that of a Japanese zen archer's as she cracks a fresh, cold egg into a small ramekin with one hand. At the same time her other hand is using the handle of a slotted spoon to stir the hot water in the pan until a gentle whirlpool forms. Dropping the contents of the ramekin into the swirling water, Lena focuses through the milky remnants of her previous poaching to make sure she doesn't lose track of the fresh egg. The whirlpool prevents the white from feathering and wraps it around the yoke.

The most difficult part for Lena of poaching an egg is leaving it the hell alone.

Christian, the Puerto Rican kid a few years younger than Lena who nonetheless is already a master of the line's grill, slides a warm plate next to Lena's station. On the plate two small, slightly charred tortillas have been hastily pressed around house-made chorizo, fresh diced jalapeño peppers, and melted cotija cheese. It looks as though one half of the tortillas have been jammed against a hard surface. The poorly executed quesadilla has been laid over a square of traditional corn cake.

Exactly four minutes and forty-eight seconds after dropping it into the water, Lena dips her slotted spoon into the pan and retrieves a perfectly poached egg. The white has hardened into a delicate sphere around what Lena knows will be an oozing, rich, golden yoke. She gently lays the tiny cloud atop the misshapen quesadilla on the plate and ladles chipotle hollandaise sauce over it. She finishes the dish by garnishing the top of the egg with a halved cherry pepper.

"Order up!" Lena calls out mechanically, setting the plate on the shelf of the window between the kitchen and the front of the house.

She's been working the egg station in the kitchen of the Ugly Quesadilla for a little over a week. It's a stopover diner in Vermont, about thirty miles outside Montpelier, so named for the intentionally malformed quesadillas that became the restaurant's signature dish decades back when it was just an uneven roadside stand on a soft shoulder of the highway. Lena stopped for lunch one day and on an utter and uncustomary whim asked if they were hiring. She mastered the "Ugly Benedict" on her first attempt, and has only become more efficient at replicating the dish dozens of times a day.

After the breakfast rush has died down, Lena takes her break out behind the diner. Sitting on an empty produce crate and drinking a cup of coffee (which has also improved in the Ugly Quesadilla since she started working the line), she thinks for approximately the millionth time about calling to check on Darren. She hasn't spoken to anyone from Sin du Jour in over a month, not Bronko, not Ritter or Dorsky. She has over a hundred unheard voice mails in her phone, most of them from Darren and only slightly fewer of them from Nikki.

The day they all flew back from Los Angeles, a part of Lena already knew she couldn't return to Sin du Jour. That evening she had a silent, more than slightly awkward dinner with Darren and turned in early. The next morning, on her way to work, Lena saw a battered 1970 Triumph Bonneville with a "for sale" sign taped to the headlight, sitting outside a garage in Long Island City. Following the first in her recent series of uncustomary impulses, she inquired inside.

The engine caused the entire bike to shake as if whoever designed it thought it might move through solid matter if it vibrated fast enough. Lena went to the nearest branch of her bank, emptied her savings account, and bought the vintage British motorcycle. She was staring at the Manhattan skyline in its dingy rearview mirror before dusk.

The Ugly Quesadilla's service door opens and Christian emerges with a grin on his young face, a plate of food balanced on his fingertips.

"Morcilla?" Lena asks him, genuinely excited.

Christian shakes his head. "Lechón. My cousin Yahir did the pig yesterday. I brought in what was left for family meal."

He lowers the plate of slow-cooked pork under her nose and waves it back and forth enticingly. Lena only briefly inhales before reaching up and snatching it from him eagerly. She grabs the fork and loads its prongs with the succulent meat and some of the arroz con gandules accompanying it.

"Gracia, pai," she says, taking her first bite.

Christian laughs. "Your white girl Spanish is coming along quick."

"Hungarian," Lena corrects him around a mouthful of pork.

He shrugs.

"It's awesome," she assures him, forking her way through the dish.

"Thanks. Hey, you want to come out with us later? We're going to this new place up the freeway. It'd get you out of that shithole motel room for a night."

"I like my shithole motel room. It's quiet. Peaceful.

And the vending machine has Andy Capp's chips. Do you know how hard it is to find those?"

Christian stares down at her blankly.

Lena shakes her head. "Thanks, though."

He spreads his arms and drops his head in a pose of mock dejection.

"All right," he says. "But I'm gonna keep asking."

Lena shrugs. "You gotta do you."

With a wink, Christian turns and walks back inside.

After he's gone, the notion to call Darren and check in returns to her. Lena can feel the phone in her front pocket, like a sudden and oppressive weight. She's felt that many times since she took off. Every time she feels it, including this time, the image of Darren staring down at her, his expression helpless and petrified, as a soldier from an ancient demon clan was trying to slit her throat flashes in her mind. Eventually the phone feels lighter in Lena's pocket.

She's not angry with Darren. She was never angry with him. But she's also done taking care of him.

Lena finishes the plate, and her coffee. She carries both back into the diner.

She hears his voice booming throughout the kitchen before she even rounds the corner from the stocking area in the back, and it stops her cold.

"Now, the thing to remember is masa lives and dies in

the kneading, all right? Water alone won't ever do it. Too little and ya got masa harina crumbles, too much and it's a damn sticky mess, and you'll never get the ratio right all by itself. You gotta work it and aerate that business to achieve the perfect texture. And y'all, corn tortillas are *all* about the texture. . . ."

At first Lena thinks they must have a television on, tuned to some cooking channel playing a rerun of one of his shows. Then she remembers there are no TVs in the kitchen, or the front of the house.

She walks back into the kitchen.

Bronko is standing at one of their prep stations, wrist-deep in a wad of dough. It's the first time she's seen him out of his chef's whites. He's wearing ripped jeans, an absurdly large belt buckle with a ceramic chile pepper on it, and a faded T-shirt bearing a half-worn-away logo of his bankrupt Deadman's Hand restaurant chain from the '90s. He's borrowed an apron from one of the cooks.

The rest of the kitchen crew has gathered around to watch him, as if they're the captive audiences for one of his old cooking shows.

"Now, once the masa stops clingin' to your hands, you're ready to—"

"Chef?" Lena blurts out in shock.

They all turn toward her, including Dave, their middle-aged day manager who currently looks starstruck.

"Jesus, Tarr, why didn't you tell me you studied under Bronko, er, Chef Luck here? You'd be runnin' the damn kitchen."

"I didn't 'study' under him, I just worked the line in . . ."

The rest of the words die on her lips. Lena feels like her brain is locking, unable to accept that Bronko is standing there in front of the Ugly Quesadilla's grill.

"What are you doing here?" she finally asks him.

Bronko smoothes his hands over the stained apron he's borrowed, then reaches for a kitchen towel.

"Someone had to keep her company on the drive up," is all he says, motioning with his heavy chin through the kitchen window.

Lena stares out at the front of the house.

Nikki is sitting at the counter, waving back at her through the kitchen window.

Now Lena is actually speechless.

"Y'all mind if I borrow her for a few minutes?" Bronko asks, removing the apron strap from around his neck.

"Sure, of course!" Dave says immediately. "Can I grab a quick selfie with you first, Chef?"

Bronko hides his distaste for the word "selfie" with the easy practice of celebrity.

"Sure thing, boss."

There are picnic tables out front. The trio finds the one

most removed from the others and settles around it.

"You followed me here?" Lena practically hisses at them both when they're alone. "Do you have any idea how creepy that is?"

Nikki frowns at Bronko. "I told you we should've called ahead."

"And I told you when folks are running away you don't give them warnin' in advance," Bronko fires back.

"Don't fucking talk about me like I'm not here!" Lena explodes. "Jesus!"

"Hey, we're sorry," Nikki says in her soothing way. "Okay? We're not, like, stalking you. But we had to find you. It's about you, not us."

"What does that mean?"

"You have to come back, Tarr."

Nikki frowns even deeper at him and his bluntness.

"We don't have time for this!" Bronko snaps at her without waiting for her reprimand.

"I've heard enough," Lena insists, rising from the picnic table bench. "You two should go."

Nikki reaches out and gently cups one of Lena's hands. "Lena, please, wait. This is serious."

She stiffens at the touch, and her eyes seem to refuse to look at Nikki, but the tone of Nikki's voice somehow manages to soften Lena. She sits back down, albeit with obvious reluctance.

"You're not safe out on your own right now," Bronko tells her. "None of us are. Not after what happened in LA. If we learned anything it's that Hell don't forget. Not ever. Now, we came through that party by the skin of our teeth, but ain't none of us going to survive without protection. Allensworth and his people are bargaining with the other side to keep us safe, but that only applies to Sin du Jour. If you're not on the line then you fall outside that protection."

"You're saying they'll come after me?"

"You can bet your knives on it, girl."

"So I don't have any choice? I have to work for you. I'm a fucking slave."

"No, a slave's a slave, and I imagine anyone who actually was that wouldn't take kindly to your exaggerations."

"Don't give me semantics, Chef!"

"Hey!" Nikki breaks in before either of them can escalate the argument further. "Chef, can you give us a second? Please?"

Bronko nods silently, pushing himself up and away from the picnic table.

They watch him walk back into the Ugly Quesadilla, then Nikki looks at Lena while Lena continues to avoid meeting her gaze.

Nikki leans back and folds her arms tightly.

"Why can't you look at me?" she finally asks.

Lena just shakes her head, squeezing her eyes closed.

"Lena—"

"I watched you die!" she unloads, tears breaking the dam of her closed eyelids. "You were gone! I know what that looks like. I've *seen* it. I watched you die covered in your own blood and come back."

Nikki stares at her, wide-eyed. "Well . . . isn't that a good thing?"

"Of course it is! But how can you be so calm about it?"

"I . . ." Nikki looks around as if she'll find the answer to the question on the grass at their feet. "I mean . . . what other choice do I have? I'm happy. Obviously. I got a reprieve I don't figure a lot of people get. I'm not going to waste it being freaked out about what happened, I guess."

"But I let you die," Lena says quietly, hands curling into fists against the tabletop as more tears come.

Nikki reaches over and strokes her fingers through Lena's hair, then leans across the table until their foreheads touch just so.

"You didn't let anything happen," she whispers. "We're not soldiers, Lena. We're chefs. You can't live the way you cook, okay? You can't control life that way, especially where we work. You just have to roll with it. Don't beat yourself up. I'm here. You're here."

Lena inhales deeply, bringing herself under control. She leans away from their brief contact.

"I'm not mad at you for what happened in LA," Nikki continues, "and I'm not mad at you for running after, okay? I get it. I know you've always felt dragged into working at Sin du Jour. I feel bad about that, and I feel worse because I'm not sorry you were. Dragged into working there, I mean. I love the place, despite everything. I always have. But for a long time I was also . . . alone. In my little kitchen with all my ovens, and now I'm not. Or at least I wasn't. And it was *so good* to have you back there with me all the time to drink and talk and joke and just generally be awesome together."

Lena doesn't respond to any of that, but she is finally meeting Nikki's eyes with her own.

"You don't have to say anything," Nikki assures her. "I know you like me too. You wouldn't be torturing yourself like this if you didn't."

"I'm sorry, all right? I'm sorry I took off without saying anything. I just couldn't . . . if I had to walk back into that place that day I was going to break apart. And then when that feeling went away I just . . . I couldn't stop going."

"You have every right to go wherever you want and do whatever you want, but what Chef is saying is true. I'm sorry, but it is. This is a dangerous time and a dangerous situation, and you *have* to come back, Lena. You just have to, at least for now. I can't . . . I don't even want to think about what might happen to you out here on your own until Allensworth is sure it's safe for all of us."

"How can he possibly protect us from something like this? And why would he? Why would we stand up against . . . all of that?"

"They need us. There's an election coming up."

Lena frowns. "What the hell do the elections have to do with anything?"

Nikki's lips tighten. "Not . . . *those* elections."

NO FEAR

With a taped-up left fist Darren shoots a jab into the heavy bag, then throws a right cross at the exact same spot. He no longer has to remind himself to follow through by rotating his hip with the punch. Darren repeats the combination again and again and again, pummeling the surface of the bag, breathing in ragged bull snarls through his nose.

"Time!" Ritter calls, staring at the stopwatch app on the screen of his phone.

Darren halts immediately, taking a step back from the heavy bag. He inhales and exhales deeply, using his taped hands to smooth the sweat from the dark beard he's been growing for the past month. It's thicker than he ever knew he could manage. He's never tried to grow his facial hair out before. The furthest Darren ever got was experimenting with a permanent five-o'clock shadow when they first moved to the city, but he shaved when another chef on the line told him it looked "gay."

It was three days after Lena blew town when Darren's mind, wholly against his will, began entertaining the possibility she might not come back. It was two days of unreturned calls later that he began to accept the possibility as a reality.

The day after that Darren went to see Ritter.

"Teach me," he'd said.

Ritter could watch creatures from Hell rise bleeding fire and brimstone with his signature passive expression, but even he'd been unable to mask his confusion.

"Teach you what?"

"How to be like you. How not to be afraid. Lena almost died because of me. One of those things . . . back in LA . . . was trying to kill her. I couldn't help her. I couldn't move."

"That's nothing to be ashamed of. Not everybody is built for combat. Fight or flight is an option for a reason."

"It's more than that! I've been afraid as long as I can remember. My whole life. I'm sick of it."

"Afraid of what?"

"Everything. Everyone. My folks, kids at school, other chefs. Everyone. Except Lena. And I didn't help her. I couldn't. I couldn't . . . *do* anything."

"You're not a soldier, Vargas. No one expects you—"

"It doesn't matter! That's not the point. I can't even stand up for her to Dorsky and the line."

"She doesn't need that."

"I know. But I do. I always do. And she always stands

up for me. I should be able to do likewise for her, whether she needs it or not. And, y'know, for myself."

"What are you asking me to do, exactly?"

"Can you just help me? Please? I'm sick of being scared. But I don't know how to . . . Lena went to war. You know? That's how she . . . but she was always braver than me, even before that."

"Vargas . . . Darren . . . you're a good guy. I can tell. But I'm not your dad. I don't know what you want me to do."

"Well, what was your dad like? What did he teach you that made you like you are?"

"Nothing you want to learn. Trust me."

"I do. I do trust you. That's why I'm asking you."

Ritter couldn't say no to that.

Not quite knowing what else to do, he's been teaching Darren how to fight. Boxing, Hapkido, knife attack defense; Darren's a good athlete and he picks up the physical training quickly. That's opened the door to talks about things like threat assessment.

"If you learn what to look for, what to *actually* be afraid of," Ritter told him a couple of weeks ago, "maybe you'll stop being afraid of everything."

He also explained to Darren that fear isn't a bad thing, or something to be extinguished. Fear is a tool, like anything else. The trick is learning to use it without it turning on you.

"Are we sparring today?" Darren asks, leaning gently against the heavy bag.

"No, you're blown up enough. Go change and go home. Grab a shower. I need to do the same."

"Tomorrow?" Darren asks with the enthusiasm and expectation of a child on Christmas Eve.

Ritter grins. He doesn't do it often, and when he does Darren feels like he's won some small victory.

"Sure," Ritter says. "We'll work on that wheel kick."

Darren walks out of Stocking & Receiving and makes the long trudge up the old industrial stairs to Sin du Jour's main level. Most of the staff has gone home for the day, as has the construction crew that's been repairing the damage the building sustained when Satan sent a demonic version of Santa Claus to destroy them all.

Bronko told them the company's parties can get a little out of control.

Anyone who's actually seen a Manhattan kitchen crew party wouldn't find that the least bit suspicious.

Sin du Jour's chefs change in an area that looks more like a high school gym's locker room than a facility in a high-end catering company's headquarters.

As he enters, Darren spots James sitting on one of the long benches in front of the rows of lockers, typing something on an iPad with a "We Are Wakanda" sticker on the back of it.

"I told you you didn't have to wait for me," Darren says, peeling off his sweat-soaked shirt and tossing it in a bin of dirty chef's whites.

James doesn't look up. "It is okay. I wanted to write my mother an email anyway. I have a lot to tell her."

"They have email in Senegal?"

James laughs. "We do in Dakar. Why does no one in America think no one in Africa uses technology? Is it the way they show us in movies?"

Darren tries to laugh, but he can't help feeling like an asshole. "Yeah, actually. I think that's exactly what it is. Sorry."

James looks up at him and smiles. "Don't worry about it. You are cute when you think you have said the wrong thing."

Darren grins. A month ago he'd have already fled the room, feeling embarrassed and ashamed.

He reaches out and gently pulls the iPad from James's hands, resting it on the bench beside him. One of Darren's taped palms strokes the perfectly smooth dome of James's scalp. The other palm cups the back of his neck. Darren leans down and kisses his lips fiercely, gripping him tightly by the head and neck. James lets himself be steered into the kiss, wilting gratefully under it.

"Just let me change and we'll go home, okay?" Darren says when their lips part.

James nods, more than a little breathless.

As Darren begins stripping the tape from his fists, he notices James rubbing his forearm across his mouth.

"Is the beard still bugging you?"

"No. You keep it nice. Just don't grow it any longer. You will look like a villain from one of those movies where Africans don't use technology."

This time Darren does laugh. He wads up the used athletic tape and tosses it into a nearby trash can.

"You want to Red Box one of those—"

In his locker, Darren's phone begins playing a song he hasn't heard in over four weeks.

The sound of it freezes his blood and drains the mirth from his face.

"What is wrong?" James asks, frowning at the change in his expression.

Darren reaches inside his locker and removes his phone, staring at the caller's name on its screen.

"It's Lena," he says.

THANES OF OLDE

Ritter stands at the base of the stairs leading up from his front door to the first level of his Canarsie townhome. He didn't need his key to open that front door, which he returned to find unlocked and ajar. He's gobsmacked, because it should be impossible to break into his house and yet it's happened twice in as many months.

The perpetrator of the first incident was a demon assassin sent from Hell, corporealized as the Easter Bunny. Ritter had to use half the magical items in his collection just to survive long enough to bash in the creature's skull.

He has no intention of repeating that kind of epic battle with this intruder.

Opening the door to the small coat closet at the bottom of the staircase, Ritter reaches inside and comes out with a pump-action twelve-gauge shotgun. He's emptied the shells loaded into the weapon of their buckshot pellets and replaced those pellets with shards of dragon bone. It's a load that will bring down a bear, or a wizard, or a wizard who has shape-shifted into a bear.

Ritter ascends the stairs, shotgun muzzle leading the way. He takes the final three steps at a run and springs around the corner.

Ritter suddenly finds himself pointing a loaded firearm at the head of his younger brother.

Marcus Thane is lounging on Ritter's treasured recliner, drinking one of his exotic rums from an ice-encumbered tumbler and watching porn on Ritter's television.

Really, really fucked-up porn.

He holds the tumbler in one hand while the other cradles a framed photograph. The picture the frame is protecting is of four men in camouflage, posing in a jungle. Ritter and Marcus are two of them.

Marcus smiles at him, a brilliant, dangerous smile that Ritter has watched seduce women and men on three different continents. Ritter is the brother who can get lost in a crowd. Marcus has always been the standout. They both have the same dark hair and dark eyes, but Marcus's features are just a little sharper, a little finer. More than that, however, is his mastery of all-day swagger where Ritter rarely lets an emotion bleed into his expression or body language.

Ritter lowers the shotgun, lips tightening just a little.

His younger brother holds up the picture frame. "I didn't know you kept this."

"Why wouldn't I?

"You aren't the sentimental type."

"Sure I am," Ritter says, the complete lack of sarcasm in his tone somehow highlighting the sarcasm in his words.

"Do you remember who took the picture?"

"Our guide's boy. Angelio, I think his name was. He had a way with the pack mules."

Marcus nods, staring up at the ceiling as if he can see the memories there. "Right. Do you think he was under some brujo's spell when he stuck that blade in my lung, or was he just on the take? Paid off by the cartel?"

"I know which would be more comforting to believe."

"Yeah. Considering you practically took his head clean off when you cut his fucking throat, I imagine one scenario would be more comforting than the other. Of course, whether he was bewitched or just a rat, his old man sure seemed not to know what was up. It's a shame we had to—"

"Whatever point you're making, Marc, you're making it badly."

"You saved my life that night."

"You saved mine, too. The jungle's like that."

"You miss it at all?"

"How'd you circumvent the seal?" Ritter asks, ignoring his brother's question.

Marcus shrugs. "It wasn't that tough. You still confuse shoplifting a few enchanted goodies from WET lockup with being some kind of warlock yourself. Took me five minutes."

Ritter folds his arms over his chest and stares down his little brother.

Marcus grins. "All right, it took me a little longer than that. Whatever."

"Are you on leave?"

Marcus tips his glass and drains its amber contents. "Permanently!" he announces.

Ritter frowns.

"How?"

His brother shrugs again.

Ritter's frown darkens.

"Marcus . . ."

"You left," he fires at Ritter, suddenly irate. "What? I can't figure out how to leave too? Am I not as smart as you?"

"I don't know. Are you? Because if you just bolted they're going to hunt you down and peel your cap like it's an old-timey photograph. And if I'm harboring you they'll probably do the same to me."

Marcus waves his glass around the apartment drunkenly. "You've got the . . . fuckin' . . . magic kibosh shit. What are you worried about?"

"I'm not set up to shade you from that kind of tracking. You know that."

"You'll come up with something."

"Look, things at Sin du Jour are popping off right now—"

"The catering company? What's 'popping off' at a catering company? Did you serve the lobster bisque cold?"

"You don't know."

"Then explain it to me."

"Stop stalling!"

Marcus sets his glass down, loudly. "Fine. Fuck it. What do you want? I'll go to a Motel 6 or some shit."

"Just tell me what happened."

"I cracked. All right? You said it would happen and it happened. I should've listened. I should've got out when you did."

In that moment Marcus almost looks like a grown-up.

"Just tell me the truth," Ritter bids him, his voice suddenly gentle. "Did you run?"

Marcus nods.

Ritter inhales deeply. "All right," he says as he exhales, his mind obviously racing. "All right. You can bunk here. I'll talk to Allensworth. We can square this. All you did was go AWOL?"

Marcus nods again.

"Nothing else happened?"

Marcus shakes his head definitively.

Ritter doesn't fully believe him, but neither does he see any percentage in pursuing the question.

OUTSIDE HIRE

Anyone of only passing acquaintance with Jett Hollinshead might be surprised to see her outside of her Louboutin heels and Chanel suits, let alone donning stained overalls to spike drywall with a nail gun as large as her torso. Anyone who knows Jett well, however, is aware that her defining quality is getting all the shit done there is to get done and by any means necessary.

"How's she coming, Jett?" Bronko asks, walking up as she stakes the last new piece of drywall to Sin du Jour's refurbished lobby walls.

"A few more days and you'll never know Santa Claus and his demonic elves rampaged through the building and tried to kill everyone in it!" she proclaims without the faintest hint of irony and the most genuine, resolved smile on her face.

It's one of the things Bronko loves about her the most. Jett has the ability to normalize even the most fantastic of situations. It's a stabilizing element to have in the world Sin du Jour services.

"Byron, I'm also thinking the entire wing could use

a face-lift, at the very least new paint. In my head I'm seeing a burnt fuchsia, with a sunburst in the lobby, possibly."

"Uh . . . yeah. Yeah, we could all do with a touch of the new, I reckon. You just . . . do what you feel, Jett. I trust you."

She beams up at him, hoisting her nail gun aloft in a salute.

Bronko can't help laughing and shaking his head.

"Excuse me, Chef Luck?"

They both turn their heads to see a statuesque woman in a sleek black and white business suit standing in the lobby. Dark, shining curls fall around a face whose features originated somewhere in the Mediterranean. She wears large-rimmed glasses with cherry-red frames and carries a vintage attaché case, alligator apparently dyed to match her glasses.

Bronko blinks rapidly and without stopping for several long seconds. Jett thinks she can actually feel the heat suddenly emanating from his every pore.

He stumbles over an attempt to respond. "I . . . uh . . . that is . . . can I help you, ma'am?"

"My name is Luciana Monrovio. I believe you're expecting me."

Bronko furrows a heavy brow beginning to perspire, then recognition lights up his eyes.

"Oh . . . ? Oh! Right! Yes! You . . . Allensworth sent you?"

Luciana nods, just once, almost a bow of her head.

"Um, pardon me," Jett chimes in. "Allensworth sent you here to do what?"

Luciana doesn't look at Jett. Her eyes are focused solely on Bronko.

"I'm your new liaison," she explains. "I'll be consulting on all your planned events, coordinating those events with sensitive personnel, and facilitating communication between your staff and Mr. Allensworth."

"Sin du Jour already has a full-time staff member with consulting, coordinating, and communicating on their résumé," Jett informs her. "And I am she."

"Er, calm down, Jett," Bronko says. "With everything that's been going on lately Allensworth wants some boots on the ground from his camp, that's all."

Jett stares down at the six-inch heels of Luciana's Stuart Weitzman pumps.

"He chose an interesting pair of boots," she says.

Luciana strides forward as if the sound of Jett's voice doesn't register. She extends a slender, manicured hand to Bronko.

"It's a pleasure to finally meet you, Chef."

Bronko rubs his hands against the front of his chef's smock before reaching out to gently take hers.

"You'll pardon me, ma'am. I suddenly feel as if every

grease splatter I've taken in the past thirty years is cling-
ing to me."

"On the contrary, Chef Luck, you look positively
camera-ready. And may I say I always enjoyed you on
television. I remember your *Good Morning, America* ap-
pearance, in particular."

"I . . . you must not have been old enough to—"

"What? Know better?"

Bronko grins and giggles like a schoolboy.

Jett clears her throat, loudly and without the slightest
pretense of subtlety.

"Byron?" she interjects. "What's happening here?
Why didn't you tell me she was coming?"

"Does Chef Luck ordinarily share interoffice policy
with maintenance workers?" Luciana asks, still looking at
Bronko even though she's addressing Jett.

"I am an executive event planner, but I'm quite sure
you already knew that, Miss Basic Corporate Undermin-
ing Tactics!"

"Jett, will ya calm down now? Don't get us off on the
wrong foot with our new go-between here. This is important stuff. You know that."

"I should apologize," Luciana says good-naturedly. "It
must be your rustic ensemble that confused me."

Jett opens her mouth to retaliate, but she's stopped
cold, literally, as Luciana finally looks directly at her.

Where she could feel the heat Luciana's presence created in Bronko, the woman's wholly ordinary gaze suddenly fills Jett with a chill that extends through her entire body, causing her conscious mind to want to retreat from the sensation and its source.

Her grip tightens around the handle of the nail gun she's holding. She feels the sudden, insane urge to—

"Jett, why don't you finish up here?" Bronko says, the sound of his voice snapping her out of it. "I'll show Miss Monrovio—"

"Luciana, please, Chef."

" . . . I'll find her some work space in the building."

Jett blinks, her brain still locked and her body shivering slightly.

"I . . . um . . . I usually take charge of orientation, Byron."

"That's all right. You've been workin' overtime lately. I've got this."

Without another word Bronko ushers Luciana down the corridor that branches off from the lobby, moving past Jett so quickly she has to jump to one side to avoid him.

She watches them go, clutching the giant commercial tool against her chest.

"What the *hell* just happened here?" she whispers to herself.

Jett was an event planner for celebrities and CEOs long before she came to work for Sin du Jour. She had no problem adjusting to a climate of monsters, magic, mayhem, and occasional demonic assassination attempts. Jett firmly believes every business landscape is essentially the same, regardless of how the topography changes. Monsters are just another feature of the valley of commerce at the end of the day. They don't scare her.

What does scare her, however, is the knowledge that outside hires, not monsters, are the most dangerous creatures in the corporate world.

PROBLEM CHILD

White Horse sits outside a local police precinct in Flushing. He's been waiting for over an hour, and he had no intention of spending any of it staring at badges and holstered Glocks. He doesn't like entering government buildings, let alone loitering inside them, and police stations are probably his least favorite government buildings.

The staples in the old man's side are still tender, as is the pierced organ beneath. He's still having nightmares about being skewered by the debris after Santa Claus hurled an exploding box wrapped like a Christmas present at Sin du Jour's lobby desk. That part isn't so bad, really. It's the part of the dream where he actually remembers what Little Dove did to save him from the hellish assassin that causes him to wake up covered in sweat.

He doesn't remember in his waking hours, and he prefers it that way.

White Horse pulls out his phone and taps the icon of the off-track betting app Little Dove keeps erasing while he sleeps. He's already placed three bets, and he's considering a fourth when Little Dove walks out of the police station.

She's carrying a yellow manila envelope and a few stapled pages of paperwork, and is looking haggard in the way people who spend the night in a jail cell do. She squints against the harshness of the sunlight and fishes inside the envelope for a pair of sunglasses, fitting them over her eyes with an irritated groan.

White Horse replaces the phone in his pocket and stands up from the bench he's been occupying. Every nerve in his torso seems to protest the action, and he curses under his breath from the pain.

"You okay?" he asks her.

"I wasn't drunk," she insists.

"Sure you were."

"I was not! It was a political protest."

"How is throwing a bottle of bottom-shelf Old Crow through a window a political protest?"

"It was the Water Board's window. All this shit on the news about the water in Flint. We've been drinking poison water on the res for as long as you've lived there."

"We're not on the res anymore."

"The water's still poison."

"The reservation isn't even in this state."

"It's the same thing!"

"Right. I'll bet that made all kinds of sense when you were drunk."

"I wasn't . . . !" she begins, then her whole being seems to relent and her shoulders slump as she sighs.

"Did you tell anyone at Sin du Jour?" she asks, sounding penitent for the first time.

"No, but I'm gonna have to. They want to arraign you next week. Bronko knows people who can squash it. You'll end up doing six months at least if they don't make it go away."

"I don't want Bronko to know."

"Tough. You want some food? You gotta be hungry."

For a moment she looks like she's about to say something shitty to him, but she either doesn't have the energy or can't come up with anything worthwhile.

In the end she just nods.

They walk down the street, White Horse holding on to one of her slight shoulders for support, until they come to a local pizza place. White Horse orders them two slices of pepperoni with jalapeños and a couple of sodas while Little Dove settles gratefully into a seat in front of a table by a large window.

Neither of them has talked about what happened during the False Idols' attack on Sin du Jour, not even to each other. But the power she unleashed that night in her fear and panic is all White Horse has thought about since.

"You know I'm no good at this kind of thing," he says, placing the food in front of her and carefully navigating his old, broken body into a seat.

"Tell me about it."

"I remember the last time you pulled a stunt like this. You were thirteen. I had to come and get you then, too."

"Because you were the only one left."

"I told you about your mom that morning."

"I was there. I remember."

"She was a good lady. She loved you. She tolerated me. She just couldn't find it to treat herself with as much kindness."

"I said I remember."

"I remember you running off. Didn't even say anything when I told you what happened. I was worried about what you'd do. To you, I mean."

"I'm not like her," Little Dove says through clenched teeth.

"I was actually relieved when they called to tell me you threw a rock through that bilagáana cop's windshield. Even if I had to pay for the damn thing."

"They let me off. Sympathy for the little Native girl whose mother just killed herself."

White Horse sighs. "This is all my fault, in a way."

"'In a way?'"

"I sensed the power in you when you were a little girl—"

40

"I don't want to talk about this."

"It lay deep and dormant. And I just thought . . . I hoped . . . it would stay there."

"I'm fine," she insists.

"You don't want to deal with what you are, with what you're becoming, so you're trying to be that pain-in-the-ass kid again. Acting out. But you can't go back. You can only go forward."

"Into what, Pop? Huh?"

White Horse rubs a hand over the grizzled contours of his ancient-looking face.

"Look, I know I ain't worth shit, all right? I never was. Not to any of my wives, not to your folks, not to you, and not to our people. I don't have the stuff Hatałii are supposed to have. But I was born with the power. Just like you. And just like you, I'm stuck with it. I don't know why. The elders didn't know why. The other Hatałii, the dedicated ones, all painted up and waving their hands like idiots, couldn't one of 'em call a spirit forth if you gave 'em their own reality television show, they definitely didn't know why. They only knew they hated my wrinkled ass. Maybe if it'd been one of them, born like this, our people'd be in better shape. But I doubt it."

Little Dove is hugging herself, near tears. "Pop, what's your point? What do you want from me?"

"I was never a grandfather like you needed, like you

deserved, but what you need now is a teacher, someone who understands what's brewing inside you. And that's me. If there was someone else, someone better, I'd get 'em for you. But there ain't. Just me. So if you'll let me, I'll do my best to be your teacher."

"Teach me to be what? A Hatałii? Medicine woman? Why the fuck would I want to be any of that?"

White Horse is already shaking his head. "Teach you how to control what you've got, and how to use it. What you use it for, what you become, will be up to you."

"Nothing is ever up to me," Little Dove says with deep disdain. "It never has been. I've always had to take care of the rest of you. I never had any choices, not one. I still don't."

"Well, then this'd be a welcome change, I expect."

Little Dove just stares at him across the table, suddenly at a loss.

"Your pizza's gettin' cold," he says a moment later when she still hasn't spoken. "Eat up. We can argue more later."

She watches him pick up his slice and take a bite. Eventually she picks a pepperoni off her own slice and pops it into her mouth.

"I was drunk," she admits.

"I know," her grandfather says. "You should switch to weed when you're stressed out. It's more mellow. Especially that busboy's stuff."

Little Dove laughs, just a little. "You really suck at being the adult."

"I know that, too," he says.

WRECKS OF GALWAY BAY

"This is an absolute bloody outrage!" Ryland shouts to the indifferent heavens in his thick brogue. "I demand satisfaction! And in the likely event I no longer possess the facilities required to experience that emotion, well then I demand *vengeance*! Empirical! Objective! Everlasting!"

"You talk funny," the tow truck driver observes with an indifference to rival that of the heavens themselves before sliding his considerable bulk into the cab of his rig.

"While *your* first language is New York Public School System, clearly!" Ryland fires back at the outside of a slammed door.

The tow truck pulls away, taking with it Ryland's battered RV with its mostly deflated tires.

He's clutching the neck of a wine bottle with scarcely an inch of comfort left at its bottom. A packet of cigarettes with three butts left inside is crushed in his opposite hand. It's all the second-generation alchemist was able to salvage from his mobile laboratory/home before it was trussed up on the flatbed that is now being driven away from Sin du Jour.

"What in the hell is going on out here?" Bronko demands.

He's standing at the service entrance of the building, knife-scarred fists on his hips.

"Are you responsible for this?" Ryland demands right back at him. "Because if so I'll remind you we've had a longstanding verbal contract vis-à-vis my domicile."

"I haven't had your rusty shit box towed in three years, Ryland, what'd possess me to do it now?"

"I'm sure I don't know, and frankly the senselessness of the act is what makes it so hurtful to me, personally."

"I'm afraid I'm responsible," a new voice says from inside the building.

Bronko turns and steps away from the service entrance. Luciana emerges, fingers clasped in front of her and a pleasant smile on her lips.

"I do apologize for any inconvenience," she continues, "but the vehicle was both an eyesore and a safety hazard. And I believe you'll agree we've had enough safety concerns as of late."

"Well then . . . madam . . . I obviously cannot argue with any of your points."

Ryland pauses, reaching back and grabbing the back of his neck to tamp down the hairs that are suddenly standing up there.

"This is very odd," he says.

"What's wrong now, Ryland?" Bronko asks.

"I find myself intensely sexually attracted to this woman," he informs Bronko without hesitation or embarrassment.

"Well now . . . that's rude as hell, but why is it odd?"

"It's odd because I drank my sexual impulses into utter and complete *abatement* years ago! I have no interest in the female gender, sexually. Or personally, professionally, politically, or conversationally, really."

Bronko turns to Luciana apologetically. "I really am sorry about him. He's brilliant at what he does and all, changin' the damnedest things into useable ingredients, but he's more or less useless at everything else in life."

Luciana continues to smile passively. "No apology required, Chef Luck."

"I am standing right here, if you'll recall," Ryland reminds them.

Bronko doesn't seem to hear him. Now that he's looking back at Luciana his attention is solely focused on her.

"Dear me . . . this is also odd," Ryland says.

"What's that?" Bronko asks absently, still smiling back at Luciana.

"I distinctly recall being very angry a moment ago, and yet now I find myself compelled to agree utterly and even gratefully with this woman I have never before met."

"Then we're all good, right?" Bronko asks, completely missing the point.

Ryland takes a full five-second swig from his wine bottle, finishing it. He lights a new cigarette and inhales half of it in less than a minute.

"My name is Luciana Monrovio, Mister Phelan," Luciana introduces herself. "I'm Sin du Jour's new executive liaison and consultant."

"I blindly accept all of that," Ryland assures her.

Luciana crooks her neck, regarding him oddly. "You know, you don't so much articulate your thoughts as narrate them."

Ryland nods. "That is a fair assessment."

"It's refreshing. That kind of real-time connection to one's processes is rare. In any event, I'll find you new quarters. *Inside* the building. All right?"

"Yes, mum."

Luciana nods, turning and walking back through the service entrance.

Ryland takes a long drag on his cigarette, squinting after her.

"Is she a mentalist or something?" he asks Bronko, who is also watching her walk away.

"She's something, all right," he says.

PASS THE AWKWARD, PLEASE

Lena's not actually surprised her key still works the lock, she's surprised by her doubt that it would.

She enters the apartment she's shared with Darren in Williamsburg since they both came to the city together. The television is on, and she can hear him laughing at whatever is playing, probably on Netflix. Lena closes the door behind her as loudly as possible and drops the small knapsack she acquired on the road.

Darren is sitting on the beat-to-hell sofa they bought from the landlord, watching *The Unbreakable Kimmy Schmidt*. She's in the middle of mentally judging his taste when she sees that James is lying on the sofa with his head cradled comfortably in Darren's lap.

"Whoa," she says, far more out loud than she intended.

They both look up and see her standing there.

"Holy shit," Darren says. "Lena."

"Hey," is the best she can come up with, and Lena thinks she should've planned more words on the way over.

Darren eases his lap from beneath James's head and stands, turning to face her. James climbs up from the sofa as well, smiling warmly at her.

"It is good to see you are okay," he says. "We were all of us worried for you, even after Chef Luck tells us he knows where you are and that you are all right."

"It's still good to see you're not dead," Darren adds.

"Yeah. Thanks. I should've called first. Or, you know, called weeks ago. Sorry about that. I . . ."

Lena trails off as she really looks at Darren for the first time. She eyes the beard, the short and spiky hair with not a drop of product in it. He's still wearing his St. Guadalupe medal, but he's even switched from boxers to skin-tight boxer-briefs.

"What's with the lumberfox porn beard?" she asks him.

Darren begins to involuntarily reach up to touch his beard, but he manages to stop himself halfway there. He lowers his hand.

"You don't like it?"

"No!" Lena says quickly. "It's . . . it works. It totally works. It's just . . . really different."

"That's kinda what I was going for."

"I told you she would like it," James says to him.

"I wasn't worried about whether you'd like it or not," Darren insists to Lena.

"He was worried whether you would like it not," James

says immediately, smiling even wider.

Lena can't help laughing.

"Jesus, this is weird." She drops her bag, hands resting on her hips as she regards them both. "So, you two are, like, a thing now? Officially?"

Darren and James look at each other, and the answer is obvious in the private grin they share, in the way their eyes mirror one another's.

"Yeah, I guess we are," Darren says.

"I should blow town more often, huh?"

The dreamy look leaves Darren's face, and he frowns at her.

Lena clears her throat. "Too soon, huh?"

He nods.

"I will leave you two to talk, okay?" James offers. "I need to write my mother an email, anyway."

He picks up an iPad off the little table beside the sofa and wanders down the lone hallway of the apartment.

Darren watches him go, waits until he hears the door to his bedroom close. He looks back at Lena.

"He writes his mom like every day. It's weird."

"You mean actually liking your mother?"

"Yeah."

Lena nods. "Fair. Listen, I don't want to crash in on you two here. I kind of feel like I've given up rights and privileges or something—"

"Don't be stupid," Darren says, interrupting her. "We've just started going out. That's all. He doesn't live here. You do. It's your home."

Lena stares at him, at more than a bit of a loss. It's not just his hair and personal grooming; his personality, his whole demeanor has changed. Darren never talked over her before, let alone with such decisiveness.

"What happened to you?" she asks, bluntly.

He doesn't answer at first, only reaches up and scratches at his beard.

"You know, my first impulse is to say how I don't know what you mean, but I know exactly what you mean. I guess the short answer is I grew up a little. It was time."

Lena is now at a total loss. "Wow. Just . . . wow. So, you're not, like, pissed at me?"

"I was," he admits. "Then I was just confused. I thought . . . I thought we were good, after Los Angeles and everything that happened and talking in that hotel room."

"We were," she assures him, genuinely. "We are. My leaving wasn't about you, dude. Really."

"I mean, that's cool, but not answering my calls or calling me back for over a month was kind of about me."

"No, that was about me. That was all about me. I couldn't . . . I just couldn't talk to anybody from here. I can't even explain why."

Some of that anger he claimed had dissipated seems to return to him. "I'm not from here, Lena. I'm from the same place you are. The exact same place. I've known you longer than anyone. It's supposed to be us against them, or at least it used to be."

"You're right, okay? It was shitty. It was a shitty, cowardly thing to do. I have no defense. I'm sorry."

That seems to deescalate him, at least for the moment.

Darren nods. "All right. Well, you should get unpacked."

"You're sure?"

"Yeah. James made this stew called mafe. It's his mom's recipe. It's lamb in a peanut butter sauce. It's pretty sick. You'll dig it."

"Cool."

Neither of them moves, however. There still seems to be a piece missing from the moment, a plug to stop it up and end it, and Lena isn't sure what that is.

Fortunately for her, the new Darren seems to have a firm handle on it. He walks around the sofa and over to her, embracing her easily, comfortably.

"Welcome home," he says.

It feels awkward to her at first, but as soon as she hugs him back her body remembers all the years they've spent as best friends.

"Thanks," she says into his shoulder. "Christ, you even smell manlier."

Still holding her, Darren giggles.

"Annnnnnnd there it is," she says, giving them both their first genuinely shared laugh of her return.

"Hey," he says, stepping back from her. "Have you called Ritter yet or talked to him?"

She blinks up at him, surprised. "I . . . what? Why? Why would I . . . ?"

"He was really worried about you. Bronko had to stop him from going after you when you split. He was going to have his whole team trying to find you. He hasn't really talked about it much, but I guess it's that soldier thing, you know? He sees you like one of his own."

Lena realizes he has no idea she and Ritter spent the night together (or spent the next morning together, several times).

She nods for far too long while she thinks of something reasonable to say. "Um . . . I haven't talked to anyone else yet, but I'll . . . I'll, like, thank him for that when I see him."

"Okay, cool. Go put your stuff away. I'll heat you up some of the mafe."

"Thanks."

Lena picks up her bag and walks toward the hallway, muttering "shit" over and over again to herself too low for anyone else to hear.

BY THE CREATURES,
FOR THE CREATURES

"First off, I want to welcome Tarr back to the line," Bronko says, addressing the entire kitchen staff in Sin du Jour's conference room.

He's standing at the head of the room's long table with Luciana lingering near the wall far behind him, watching. Lena is seated at the opposite end, once again wearing the cartoon cake company logo on the breast of her smock.

Assembled around both sides of the table in their chef's whites, the rest of the line mock applauds her. Lena does her best to grin and bear it, but mostly she's trying to simultaneously avoid looking at Tag Dorsky, Sin du Jour's sous-chef, and Darren, the best friend and roommate she abandoned.

Dorsky is one of two men she slept with before leaving town without so much as a word. Thus far she's managed to avoid the other man entirely, and at the very least she's avoided any one-on-one time with Tag.

For his part, Dorsky is acting as though nothing happened, between them or otherwise. He just sits there with that cocky, perpetual half-smile on his face, surrounded by his three chief kitchen cronies.

Darren, on the other hand, is having much more trouble hiding a variety of emotions inspired by Lena's renewed presence. But at least James, who is seated next to him, so close the arms of their chairs are touching, pleasantly distracts him.

"It's election time again, kids," Bronko announces.

Everyone except Lena and Darren groans.

"Didn't they just have those, for chrissakes?" Dorsky asks.

"We've got one of the frontrunners comin' to town for a three-week fireside tour."

"Democrat or Republican?" Lena asks wryly, although she's already gotten hip to the fact they're *not* talking about the American presidential race, or any election in the everyday human world.

"That's funny, Tarr," Bronko says. "That's why we missed you so damn much around here, that earthy sense of humor."

"So, is someone going to explain to the newbies what these elections you're talking about are for?" Darren asks.

"Sure, Vargas," Bronko says. "And I love this new forceful thing you're doing now that you've become a . . . whadda-you-call-'em? A bear."

"I'm not a bear, Chef."

"What was that?" Dorsky asks. "All I heard was 'rrrraaarrr!'"

Seated beside him, Rollo and the rest of the line laugh, even James, who nudges Darren playfully.

"Fuck off, Dorsky," Darren says.

Sin du Jour's sous-chef blinks his surprise at Darren while the others "ooh" and "ahh" after the surprising display.

"All right, all right! Enough grab-ass!" Bronko orders. "To answer your question that was phrased like a statement, Vargas, every four years, in line with the elections y'all have grown up watching, the *Sceadu* also elect a new president."

"What's a *Sceadu*?" Lena asks.

"It's the shadow government," Nikki informs her. "If you think of all the nonpeople we cook for like a high school, the *Sceadu* is the student council."

"And how does that even work?"

"Everybody is pretty much allowed to tend to their own business," Bronko explains. "Goblins, half-and-halfs, demons, what-have-you. A lot of 'em have their own . . . whatever . . . realms that aren't strictly part of our world, and that's all separate from this. But a lot of 'em live here and they all do business here. Inevitably their business, or whatever, is going to bleed over into each other's backyards. When that happens, the *Sceadu* mediates and arbitrates and all that. They also set policy for the folks we cater to about how they all conduct themselves in public, so none of this shit ends up on TMZ."

"I thought Allensworth and his people did that," Lena says.

"Mister Allensworth represents the interests of humanity at large among the various supernatural factions," Luciana says before Bronko can respond to that. "Ours is a diplomatic charter, not a legislative one. We don't set policy for those factions."

Lena points at Luciana. "Who is she again, Chef?"

"She works for Allensworth, and she'll be actin' as a go-between with us and him."

"Since when?" Dorsky practically demands. "We've never needed that before."

"And shouldn't Jett be here for this, Chef?" Nikki asks. "She never misses warrooms."

"It's been decided," Luciana interjects, "you'll scale back the . . . well, scale of your events. In light of recent incidents it's better your exposure is limited, for your own safety. Simply provide the main service required of you and that's all."

Bronko steps in before any of them can question Luciana further. "Anyway. It's all as big a mess as regular-ass human politics, I'm sure, but all we have to worry about is the food. We've got the very first human candidate to run for the

Sceadu presidency comin' to New York next week—"

"What's his name?" Nikki asks.

Bronko consults some papers on the table in front of him. "Uh ... Enzo. Enzo Consoné. I guess he started out as some kind of motivational speaker and confidant to the rich and powerful—demons, CEOs, demon CEOs—and worked his way up—"

"He's a con man," Luciana interrupts, her pleasant tone abandoning her for the first time. "A cheap trickster who smiled and screwed his way to where he is. He'll never win the presidency of the *Sceadu*."

Lena raises a brow at the sudden, inexplicable outburst. She glances over at Nikki, who looks back with the same bemusement.

Lena is about to comment when she witnesses something else inexplicable. Around the table, all the men are nodding their heads in agreement with Luciana's words. It's not so much that they're nodding; it's the *way* they're nodding, with their expressions detached from the gesture, almost as if it's a reflex action.

"Well, the election'll be what it'll be," Bronko says. "The candidate is going to be givin' two big speeches at two events, a week apart. We're doing both of 'em, obviously. There's going to be one for the elementals and one for the bigwigs from the goblin hierarchy and the clued-in humans."

"Why do they always have to do the elementals here?" Dorsky whines. "You know what a Mongolian cluster-fuck those gigs always are."

"That's why we get paid the big bucks," Bronko reminds him. "Besides, most of us have had more experience dealin' with elemental clientele than we did last go 'round. I'm confident y'all will pull it off smoothly."

Dorsky coughs into his hand. "Bullshit!"

"You're extra saucy today, Tag," Bronko observes. "Are your tender places still hurtin' over Tarr there being gone for so long?"

No one laughs at that. The rest of the line sitting on either side of Dorsky all drop their gaze or find something very interesting on the walls or ceiling to contemplate.

Dorksy just smiles, breezily, looking totally unperturbed.

"I'm all good, Chef," he says. "Happy to have her back on the line. We're going to need all the help we can get."

"Good. I've written out temporary menus here for y'all. We'll firm 'em up as we talk individual assignments and schedules. Nikki, I'll get with you on dessert separately. Any more questions for now?"

Lena raises her hand and Bronko gives her the nod.

"Yeah," she says, dropping her arm. "What the hell is an 'elemental'?"

EARTH, AIR, WIND & FIRE

"Is good you come back," Boosha says to Lena, patting her cheek with a withered hand. "You belong here. This I know."

"Yeah, sure," Lena says, trying to ignore the cloying, antiseptic smell of the ancient woman's apothecary.

She hadn't realized how much she'd gotten used to it while working at Sin du Jour, but being away for over a month and stepping back into the dangerously cluttered, musty space has definitely reminded her.

"And you," Boosha addresses Darren, who's lingering near the door behind Lena, "your spirit . . . is changed. Is louder, bigger. Is good. You were much inside when first I met you. Too much. Is good to see. But you come here more often! I have not seen you since this one leaves."

"Can you download us on the elementals already please, Boosha?" Darren asks, impatient. "We have a lot of work—"

"Don't rush!" Boosha snaps at him. "Spirit bigger, is good. But stay nice boy you are. Don't rush people. Is rude. Don't be rude."

Lena drops her head, trying not to grin and failing.

Darren frowns at the back of her head, knowing full well that she did.

Boosha fetches one of her large, dusty, antique tomes and hoists it up onto the lectern that looks like it was carved from a tree in a Tolkien novel. She opens the book and flips through its stiff, nearly petrified pages. She stops when she comes to a faded two-page illustration; it's a tableau of different creatures all intertwined with each other and performing various tasks.

"Elementals once made this world turn, just for you. They were not born to protect nature, as many of your people think. They were born for you. They protected your people from power of raw elements. Controlled those elements. Guided them. For countless ages. Then your people learn to protect themselves from nature. Then your people learn to control nature. Then you learn to kill nature. Somewhere along way elementals are forgotten. They retreat into the earth, into the sea."

Boosha points at a section of one of the pages on which what looks like a lizard made of fire is painted. It might've once been a vibrant red, but age has turned it a pale pink-orange.

"Salamanders are great creatures of flame. Not very smart. Ruled by instinct and impulse. They are drawn to fire. They take it in themselves. It makes them bigger, stronger. But it burns down too quickly. Mostly now they stay near the warmth of this world's middle, deep down."

Her frail fingertip with its long, cracked nail traces down the page to a cluster of tiny figures with bushy beards, encumbered by what look like pieces of armor fashioned from rock.

"Gnomes are little ones. Great craftsmen. Can build most anything. Once they made the mountains and valleys and plains, shifting the ground beneath your feet as was needed. Now they mostly live in deep holes hiding from humans and fighting with other little ones forced to go below."

The opposing page in the book features a fishlike creature with tiny, withered bipedal arms being encircled by strong gusts of wind. Lena squints as Boosha runs her fingers over the illustration. She realizes the wind has been rendered with subtle faces in it.

"Undines are of the sea. You call them mermaids. But are not like your fairy tales. They have no . . . how to say . . . human parts? All fish. Sylphs are of the air. They have no bodies. Strange creatures. Intelligent, yes, but not in a way we will ever truly understand, I think."

"That's all very amazing and weird and . . . whatever," Lena says, sounding very tired all of a sudden. "But I'm confused about one thing. And the fact it's only one thing I'm confused about is just . . . wow."

"What is one thing?" Boosha asks patiently.

"If we don't need them anymore, why is this guy running for president of the *Sceadu* giving some kind of rally for the elementals?"

"Is mostly for show. Ceremonial. But is also smart, and necessary. Elementals possess great power, even if they have forgotten. They could cause much chaos for this world if they chose. Is good to appease them. And as some of the oldest of us all they have voice in the choosing of new exaltated."

"Exalt . . . I thought they were electing a president?" Lena asks.

Boosha shrugs, closing the book with a grunt of effort. "'President,'" she says, enunciating each syllable carefully, "is what is called now, here. Was different in ages past."

"How many ages have you lived through, Boosha?" Darren asks.

"Many. Some I remember more fondly than others."

"So, is this a regular thing you do?" a new voice asks from the apothecary's doorway.

Luciana is standing there, watching them.

Lena and Darren both turn to look at her, startled, while Boosha attends to her book as if she hasn't taken notice of the woman.

"Hold these little tutorials, I mean," Luciana clarifies.

"Ummmm... yeah, Boosha's kinda like Wikipedia for ... I mean ... stuff there's no Wikipedia for," Darren tells her.

"She obviously knows quite a lot," Luciana says pleasantly.

"Know what you are," Boosha hisses under her breath, still not acknowledging the woman.

Lena's brow furrows as she looks from Sin du Jour's new executive to its not entirely human elder.

Luciana smiles tightly. "Very quaint. I'll leave you to your ... whatever."

Her gaze lingers for a moment on Boosha hunched over her lectern, then Luciana turns and walks away.

"That was weird," Darren says, bluntly, after she's gone.

"Yeah, because that word still means things here." Lena takes a deep, stabilizing breath. "So, Boosha... what do elementals eat, then?"

"(mumbles). Yeah. Booshka kinda like Whoopda-lar. I mean . . . stuff those one Wilipeth lee?" I got childish. . . .

She obviously knows a game. "Ie?" Lux mau says pleasantly . . . .

"Now what you are," Boosha hisses under her breath, still not acknowledging the woman.

Lux's brow furrows as she looks from him all four new creature to its not entirely human elder.

Luciana smiles tautly. "Very quaint. I'll leave you to your . . . palaver.

The elder lingers for a moment on Boosha hunched over her terrain, then I gotta burn and walks away.

"That was weird," Luciana says bluntly, after she's gone.

"Yeah, because that word still means 'mine' now."

Luxx takes a deep, stabilizing breath. "So, Boosha, . . . what are please she eat them?"

THE MAD PASTRY CHEF

"Ice!" Nikki calls to Lena over the loud hissing of the machine. "Everything has to be frozen with liquid nitrogen first!"

"For the salamanders?" Lena asks.

Nikki nods animatedly, an excited grin plastered on her face.

She's wearing insulated gloves that make her hands appear four times larger than they actually are, and safety goggles that make her look like a mad scientist. Nikki is cradling a thick hose with a stainless-steel nozzle at the end. The other end of the hose is connected to a refrigeration unit almost as tall as she is, with two tanks full of liquid nitrogen welded to each side like pontoons.

Lena's hunched over a freestanding prep island with a wineglass in one hand and a bottle of red in the other, watching her.

"Should I be worried about what's going to happen here in a second?"

Nikki blinks at her through the goggles.

"Why do you ask?"

Lena glances back at the entrance to Nikki's small pastry kitchen.

Cindy, Moon, and Hara from Sin du Jour's intrepid Stocking & Receiving Department have barricaded the small archway by hanging thick welding blankets over it.

Moon is kneeling behind a steel drum he rolled into the kitchen (where Hara had to stand it upright for him). The little man has practically folded himself in half, as if preparing for his plane to go down. His body is curled around a fire extinguisher.

"Are you fucking with me, or is all this really necessary?" Lena asks them.

"Well," Cindy begins, "the last time Betty Crockerstein there went buck-wild with liquid nitrogen—"

"You weren't there!" Moon shouts at Lena in abject horror. "You didn't *see* it!"

"You're all totally exaggerating right now!" Nikki insists.

There are dollops of tawny-brown ice cream plated in front of her, the largest portions Lena has ever seen. Each stainless-steel platter must have five gallons of the dessert atop it, sculpted into perfect spheres. Each one has been drizzled with waterfalls of a maroon sauce as thick as preserves.

"Salamanders like meat," Nikki explains to Lena. "Organs, in particular. But they like them sweetened. So I made a foie gras ice cream with a plum sauce."

"I thought the whole point was to freeze it into ice cream with the nitrogen?" Lena asks.

"Usually, but salamanders are, like, literally made of fire. They'll melt or roast food before it ever gets close to them. So I'm freezing everything!"

"Which, in theory, is the opposite of blowing stuff up," Moon observes, and Nikki glares at him for it.

"Here we go!" she announces with glee, cranking back on the nozzle of the hose.

The tanks whir and the hose hisses like a chorus of snakes. White frost sprays forth, consuming the first mountain of ice cream and its steel platter. Nikki cackles madly as she aims and fires the hose at each gargantuan dessert, freezing them solid.

Lena sips her wine. She's far more amused than afraid. Behind her, Ritter's team cowers behind their barricades.

"Damn that's fun!" Nikki proclaims when she's done, cinching the nozzle closed tightly over the mouth of the hose.

She's created half a dozen ice fossils the size of engine blocks.

"I'm also making sticky mango rice balls for the salamanders, which you *have* to try before I blast them!" she tells Lena. "They're like beach balls!"

"You're having way too much fun, you know that, right?"

"No such thing," Nikki insists.

THE WOMAN WHO KNEW
TOO MUCH

Boosha has spent the majority of her evening angrily puttering around her apothecary needlessly rearranging three curio shops' worth of items in frustration. She's been at it pretty much nonstop since her dissertation on the elementals was interrupted.

"Good evening, Boosha."

She is truly tired of Luciana Monrovio seeming to suddenly coalesce in her doorway.

"What you want?"

Luciana takes a few steps inside the room, one hand delicately swinging her vintage attaché case the color of blood.

"I'm curious . . . how old are you?"

"Old enough to know is rude to ask this question."

"Of course. Pardon me."

Boosha steps beside her lectern, one wrinkled hand deftly stroking its hand-carved wooden spine.

"I know why you come here. Why they send you."

Luciana smiles warmly. "Of course you do. Because, as

you said before, you know what I am."

Boosha nods once, sharply.

"It's funny," Luciana continues, "I can't quite place your origins. I'm very good at that, usually. You're not human. You're not demon."

"Am many things. Have seen many things."

"Yes, that's what you do here, isn't it? You impart the knowledge of your considerable years to Chef Luck and his staff."

"They are much like children to you and I," Boosha says, and there's an obvious and unbidden affection in her tone. "They have so little time in their skins, to see and to know. Most of them will never understand their own world as it truly is. Yet the ones here have seen, do know, even if they cannot understand. I try to help them. They are kind. Mean well."

"That's very sweet. It's very . . . motherly."

"What your purpose is here? Truly?"

"I think you know. I had to treat you like a doddering old biddy, naturally, so Chef Luck and his staff would never suspect you posed a threat to me, but it's obvious you're the sharpest knife in this particular kitchen."

"I will not let you hurt these people."

"That's your last word on the matter?"

"No."

With that, Boosha spits on the floor at her feet.

"Last word," she pronounces.

Luciana's smile never falters.

"Very well, then," she says.

Luciana hefts her attaché case and plants it flat atop stacks of old tomes near the door. She demurely removes her wide-rimmed eyeglasses and folds the stems, slipping them into the breast pocket of her dark, sleek suit. She reaches out and presses her thumbs against the clasps securing the two halves of the bloody business accessory.

Boosha's eyes narrow into serpentine slits, watching her. The muscles of her hand tense against the body of the lectern, and suddenly the grip of a black steel stiletto is filling her palm.

Luciana pops the attaché case open, just a crack, and immediately the shadows inside begin spilling out in thick waves of black that seem to flow on the air like ink in the absence of gravity.

She turns her gaze away from the case to regard Boosha, and that unwavering, professional smile suddenly turns sinister.

"All right," Luciana says, brightly. "Let's begin."

PART II

X'S AND O'S

WHO ONCE MADE THE
EARTH MOVE

The strip of Bed-Stuy waterfront is an unfinished jigsaw puzzle of gentrification; multimillion-dollar developments guarded by Whole Foods standing abreast of each shiny new complex like sentinels, broken up by barren lots, faded tenements, and crumbling industrial ruins.

In the glass banquet hall of one such ever-rising steel condominium, Sin du Jour is awaiting the arrival of the campaign event's elemental guests. Allensworth and his entourage of shadowy, nameless government agency cronies are already there, milling about the edge of the large moon pool that runs right under two giant bay doors set into the far wall of the space, and out into the East River.

The only other people to have arrived are a contingent of half a dozen obviously homeless people seated around one of the many velvet-draped tables in front of a small speaker's stage. Lena can only guess it's some kind of outreach program, or a prop in the political speech being made this evening, although she wouldn't have guessed such issues mattered in the subcutaneous world of the supernatural.

She is currently watching them quizzically, not because of their tattered layers of clothing or unkempt faces, but because they're apparently not being allowed to eat. Filling the table in front of them is a fast food feast from Henley's. There must be hundreds of Chicken Nuggies in their cardboard boxes with tiny plastic caps of Big Top sauce formed into four-foot pyramids. Double Udder sandwiches wrapped in foil are piled just as high and surrounded by plastic containers of Clown Noses, the roasted red potatoes Henley's offers in lieu of French fries.

Lena can see the poor people shifting in their seats, eyeing the food both nervously and wantonly, and occasionally casting their desperate gaze at Allensworth's people. It just seems flat-out cruel to her, and unnecessarily so.

She is staffing a buffet table of the miniaturized dishes they've designed for the gnomish contingent. Bronko's coin-sized bento boxes with chopsticks half the length of threading needles are meticulously arranged in kanji symbol patterns. Beside those are ratatouille teaspoons, and micro-terrines of mushroom and dandelion root.

A new group of men enters the space, all of them wearing expensive three-piece suits. From a distance each one of their heads seems to Lena to sparkle in the light. As they approach Allensworth and his people, Lena realizes the new arrivals all have the slickest hair, the whitest teeth, and the shiniest skin she's ever seen. They're like Brooks Brothers mannequins made flesh. All of them seem to have permanent, brilliant smiles plastered on their faces.

Allensworth greets each one of them warmly, shaking hands with a mechanical detachment.

A few seconds later, one of the polished men breaks away from Allensworth's glad-handing session. He crosses over to Lena's station. She has to consciously remind herself to smile professionally and not stare at the freakishly manicured individual with bewilderment.

The man stares down at the doll-sized cuisine silently. Lena opens her mouth to inform him (cordially, of course) the dishes are that size because they've been prepared for gnomes. However, she never gets the words out because the man's left cheek suddenly drops from his face.

There's no blood or gore or shriek of pain. A portion of the man's face simply falls away from the rest of him, leaving a dark, dry depression. He doesn't react to the event at all, but Lena does, taking an involuntary step back, her eyes wide and filled with horror as she watches the man begin to literally fall apart. More pieces of his face and skull fall away, then his neck and shoulders, clothing included, all of it crumbling in symmetrical chunks.

Darren is suddenly there, hands on her biceps, stabilizing her as subtly as he can.

"Chill out," he whispers. "They're the gnomes."

And so they are. Lena manages to shift her gaze from the man on the other side of the table who is now just a waist and a pair of legs to the table itself. Dozens of tiny, bearded, bipedal figures flit gracefully down onto the tabletop, each one wearing a patch of the man's skin or clothing, or a fully functioning organ like an eye, as an oversized hat. Mechanical parts are affixed to their limbs, curved prongs and interlocking joints fashioned to connect with one another.

The gnomes stand on the table in front of Lena and Darren, chatting in voices too low for their words to register in human ears. They pick up the bento boxes and chopsticks and begin to snack as they converse among themselves.

"Boosha failed to mention this part," Lena says tightly, as gently as possible shaking free of Darren's hands.

He quickly steps away from her, arms going stiffly and self-consciously to his sides. "I think this is, like, a recent innovation."

"Ritter told me about those gnomes his team ran into in Wales, but he didn't say they could make goddamn human androids."

Dorsky's head suddenly appears between them as he leans in and whispers, "CEO gnomes."

"Fucking hell," she hisses at him, startled. "What?"

"They're just like people," he says. "Only smaller. Not all gnomes are created equal. Some forage in the dirt, some sell off endless streams of Silicon Valley start-ups. Whose vote d'ya think a dude running for *Sceadu* president would want to court?"

The gnomes savage half the contents of the buffet table in minutes. Lena bolts to the kitchen attached to the banquet space for reloads. She finds Bronko back there, leaning over a gas range where a towering pot of emulsified vegetables is steaming.

"Where're we at?" he asks her, sounding wearied and tired.

"Guests are arriving. I need more mini-apps."

Bronko silently waves an arm at a stainless-steel shelf where platters of the gnomish dishes are waiting for her.

"You okay, Chef?" Lena asks him.

"Haven't been sleeping great," is all he tells her.

When Lena returns with the platters, she finds everyone gathered around the moon pool. Its waters are currently bubbling furiously, as if a great submarine is preparing to emerge from the depths.

Instead, seven gray-green bodies break above the surface of the pool. Covered in gleaming scales and with hammer-shaped heads, they appear as large as full-grown human beings, and even have a vague human shape. Sets of six-inch gills pulsate on both sides of each thick neck, and the undines even have stubby, atrophied arms dangling from their chests.

Heavily modified Segway personal transporters are submerged at the foot of a concrete ramp leading out of the pool. Each one of the conveyances has a vertical, cylindrical tank bolted to where the rider is meant to stand. The undines swim up to the personal transporters and carefully wriggle the fishtail halves of their bodies into those customized tanks. Mechanical braces lock into place, holding them upright, and one by one they wheel up the ramp.

As they exit the pool, Mr. Mirabel, Sin du Jour's elderly, air tank–encumbered busboy, offers each one a large plastic bib, or "fibs" as they've come to be known around the Sin du Jour kitchen (for "fish bibs," although Jett reminded the staff the politically correct term is "pharynx receptacle"). They're actually two plastic bags that fit over the undines' gills, connected by a collar ring.

When the last of the undines has rolled away from the edge of the pool, the bay doors retract and the bow of a nondescript fishing boat is guided into its waters. Its hull is scrawled with Mandarin characters. On its deck, a large shipping container is wheeled toward the bow under the power of two figures completely obscured by the reflective fire proximity suits they wear. The attendants wedge the container as close to the tip of the bow as possible and pull the latches securing its front entry doors.

The doors fly open as two gargantuan, four-legged reptiles with flaming scales burst forth from within the shipping container. The curved claws of their front feet grasp the bow of the vessel like grappling hooks, pulling their bodies overboard and dropping into the moon pool like two Cadillac cars driven off a cliff.

The surface of the water sizzles, and steam rises in thick sheets from it. When the salamanders' long snouts first break above the water, they're black and extinguished, smoke still trailing from their scales. In the next instant, however, as the air hits them anew, those scales burst aflame, burning bright and hot and red.

The next thing Lena sees is Nikki, fearlessly wheeling a large stainless-steel cart burdened with her frozen treats toward the pool. When they see the food approaching, the salamanders paddle to the moon pool's edge and hang their long snouts over it, waiting.

When Nikki has angled the cart close enough, the first salamander lifts its head, opens its maw, and a burning tongue whips out. The lash of flame encircles one of the frozen blocks of foie gras and reels it into the creature's mouth. Steam immediately shoots from the elemental's every orifice, and the fire blazing around its snout dims noticeably for several moments.

When it swallows, the steam jets die down and the flames rise high from its snout once more. The salamander rumbles in what Lena can only hope is satisfaction. It seems sated, however.

She spots Dorsky standing by the entrance to the kitchen, watching the scene with mild amusement. Lena briefly abandons her station and walks over to him. They haven't traded a meaningful word since her return, and his indifference has rapidly gone from being a relief to annoying the absolute piss out of her.

"So, are dragons a real thing too?" she asks him.

He shrugs, not looking away from the feasting salamanders and Nikki. "Probably. I don't know. We've never had to cook for them."

"Look, when are we going to have the awkward conversation?" she asks suddenly.

"About what?"

There's no sarcasm in his voice, and no hesitation.

Lena wants to kick him in his liver and feel the poisonous sack burst inside his body cavity.

"Fine," she says. "Just be . . . you."

Lena walks back to her buffet station, not quite boiling, but at least simmering.

The glass ceiling of the banquet hall is one large, open

skylight. The night above is calm and cool for this time of year. The stars are unobscured, at least for the first part of the evening. As she stands at her station, muttering unkindly under her breath and staring up, Lena sees a distortion through the skylight. It's almost like the jet engine of a plane blurring the background.

She feels the wind rise and then turn violent a few moments later. Great gusts suddenly billow down from the skylight, causing tablecloths to waft and even knocking over centerpieces and empty chairs. The wind pouring down through the skylight eventually takes on a faint color, almost like milky smoke. Lena begins to make out several distinct and separate patches of the misty stuff.

If they're not the sylphs, the air elementals, then Lena is a line cook at TGI Friday's.

It's like watching ghosts in some old cartoon, wisps of shapeless, formless white swirling around in circles above all of their heads. Eventually they fall into formation, like birds, and streak across the room.

The sylphs enter the homeless delegation seated at their front table loaded down with Henley's fast food. The wispy forms disappear through nostrils, ears, and mouths. Each weary body is thrown back against its chair, convulsing for several moments before snapping back into a perfect, calm stillness. A new awareness dawns on each smudged face.

The thing that shocks Lena the most is how quickly she's able to realize, understand, process, and accept what's happening. Her Sin du Jour training has far exceeded simple culinary craft. She expects Allensworth to walk over and gland-hand the sylphs, now firmly in control of their homeless hosts.

Instead the air elementals tear into the Henley's fare like a pack of feral, starved dogs.

As she watches them wordlessly, ravenously, and without a single semblance of etiquette devouring the cheap fast food, Lena thinks back to something Chef Luck said to her. It was during her first day at the company. Chef compared the world they serviced as watching something foreign and exotic on National Geographic. That's what this feels like to Lena. These are beings that obviously exist without form, without any notion of the physical, suddenly inhabiting physical bodies and experiencing their sensations and pleasures.

Lena imagines she would probably act the same way.

She just hopes they don't all start fucking each other too.

It's all she can do to ignore the nauseating sight of the possessed bodies gorging themselves with both hands. It's hardly the evening's most off-putting image, however. As she watches, the undines dip their heads into long, gilded troughs of emulsified frog meat or algae, as a vegetarian option ("We have to prep a vegan option for fish?" Dorsky had asked several times throughout the week).

The liquid fare is cycled through their gills and ejected into the plastic bags of their fibs. That part's not so bad, but when Mo attempts to help one undine remove its nearly full fib bag and it rips open, marinating him in recycled fish food, Lena almost retches.

Pacific, on the other hand, bursts out laughing.

The elementals feast and commiserate for the next hour. They all seem to be able to communicate with one another, except for the sylphs, who everyone, elemental and human, seems to patently avoid.

Eventually, Allensworth mounts the stage and removes a microphone from its stand.

"If I could draw your attentions from all the lovely food and drink this evening, I'd just like to thank the esteemed representatives of our four elemental enclaves that made the arduous journey tonight. As you all know, the *Sceadu* is ready to sit a new four-year president. We're gathered to hear from one of the front-runners this evening, the first independent candidate in the election's history to win the nomination from the Order of Shadows, not to mention the first human to ever seek the *Sceadu* presidency. It's my duty to welcome him to the stage now ... Enzo Consoné!"

Lena isn't positive, but she thinks she detects hesitance in Allensworth's usually smooth, unperturbed delivery. If she didn't know better, and she realizes in that moment she doesn't, Lena would almost think she detected a note of disdain, too.

When Enzo Consoné takes to the stage, Lena is surprised by how young he appears. She'd pictured a more venerated man, but Consoné looks to be barely out of his twenties, if that. He's clean-shaven, aging his face down further, and his short black hair has been left unsullied by any product. He wears a dark suit with no tie, but doesn't do that atrocious I-forgot-to-button-my-top-shirt-button thing Lena hates.

Another man, a full head taller and a great deal bulkier, takes up position in front of the stage, folding his hands in front of him and moving his eyes over the whole of the room. He's obviously the candidate's personal security. He looks like a hard individual to Lena, with his stony eyes, military-cropped hair, and old-school mustache. Oddly, his hips appear even broader than his shoulders.

No one except Lena seems to notice him.

Their eyes are all on Enzo Consoné.

Nikki presses a hand to her chest as if she's pledging allegiance to a very sexy flag. "Every pair of panties I own is now ruined."

"Me too," Darren agrees.

Lena looks at both of them with open disdain.

Sure, she thinks, he's kind of hot. But no more so than any actor wearing scrubs on a network TV show about doctors.

Consoné kneels then, like a supplicant, or an impassioned football coach about to give the big speech. He cups the microphone in his hand, holding it against his lips as his eyes slowly scan every person and creature in the vast space surrounding the stage.

"You . . . who once moved the Earth," he breathes heavily and solemnly into the microphone. "I bow to you all."

"I want to fuck his voice," Nikki whispers.

"I want his voice to fuck me," Darren whispers back.

"Will you two shut up!" Lena snaps at them. "What is *wrong* with you?"

She can see by their expressions that they either can't hear her or aren't listening.

Lena looks around at the elementals. Each group has fallen silent and still. Even the sylphs, contained in the bodies of their gorging homeless hosts, have stopped endlessly consuming fast food to watch the candidate.

Consoné rises, slowly pacing the front of the stage, each movement deliberate and purposeful.

"Every four years a new hopeful stands here before you, offering platitudes, offering respect for your past, honoring what you *once* were. I would never profane your might with such insults, such empty, meaningless lip service. No, I am here to honor and pay homage to *the gods that you are* as I have knelt before you today!"

A chorus of gnomish voices cheers him then. In the tanks of their Segways, the undines loudly thrash their tails in the river water, making what noise they can with their thin lips. The salamanders swing their broad snouts back and forth and roar, their nostrils belching smoke and flame.

Consoné leaps from the stage then, landing gracefully beside the grease-soiled, wrapper-covered table occupied by the sylphs' indigent hosts. Casting his microphone aside, the candidate reaches out and grasps the nearest one, a bearded middle-aged man, by his matted and mangy head. Consoné crushes his mouth over the crumb-covered hole in the man's bushy beard, breathing into it as if attempting to resuscitate him.

"My Christ," Lena practically gags.

"This should not be hot, and yet—" Darren begins.

"Totally is," Nikki finishes for him.

Consoné repeats the action with each host around the table, breathing the air of his own lungs into whatever essence the sylphs consist of that has taken control of these people.

When he's finished, each food-covered face is staring

wide-eyed and adoringly after him.

The rest of the elements roar, cheer, and splash their approval.

Consoné picks up the microphone and leaps back onto the stage in one catlike bound.

"When I'm confirmed as president of the *Sceadu,* you *will not* be forgotten as you are after every one of these elections! You are owed fealty from the humans you protected in the infancy of their race! You are owed reverence for the power over their world you hold within you! Above all, you are owed domain! I say to the salamanders, no longer will you be the tools of coal barons! I say to the Gnomi, all that exists below the surfaces of this Earth is yours! I say to the undines, your waters shall be purified and borders preserved and respected by every great government of the human world! I am your servant, and my task is not done until I realize each and every one of these vows!"

With that thunderous conclusion, Consoné literally drops the mic. He spreads his arms wide and throws his head back as the room explodes into exaltation. The gnomes pound the tabletops and floor with any object they can seize. The bodies of the salamanders become infernos, blasting flame high enough to reach the open skylight of the hall. The sylphs flee their human hosts, swirling their illusory forms into one great midair tornado that sends gales slamming every corner of the room.

Lena, Darren, and Nikki are actually forced to take cover behind one of their own buffet tables, crouching low and holding it in place.

"This is fucking crazy!" Lena yells over the chaos and commotion of it all.

"I know!" Nikki shouts back with genuine enthusiasm. "I would *so* vote for this guy!"

Lena stares deadpan at the grin plastered sappily on Nikki's face.

When Lena manages to peer over the refuge of the buffet table, Enzo Consoné has left the stage. She only catches a glimpse of his bodyguard's broad shoulders as they disappear into some sequestered antechamber of the building, away from the rest of the banquet hall.

The elementals are still clamoring as if calling Elvis back onstage for an encore.

In the midst of it all, Lena has the most absurd thought, yet with a clarity she can't deny: even for a world as screwed up as the one in which she's found herself, what just happened is *not* normal.

THE GRIND

"What the fuck do you mean I'm not *allowed* in the kitchen?"

Lena is standing in the lobby corridor outside of what used to be the large open archway leading into Sin du Jour's main kitchen. That empty space is now suddenly and inexplicably filled with an ornate locked security gate. Thick wrought-iron bars forged into the twisting shape of barbed vines are welded into two frames.

Luciana just smiles what Lena perceives as that patronizing smile, hands clasped in front of her around the handle of her attaché as if the case is a shield bearing her standard.

"You're not disallowed from the kitchen," she assures Lena. "That's ridiculous. You've been reassigned. You're going to assist Miss Glowin in the pastry kitchen."

Lena is ready to implode like a neutron star and swallow Luciana in her wake. "'Assist?'"

"*In addition,* access to sensitive areas in Sin du Jour is now restricted to staff specifically assigned to those areas. The personnel in the main kitchen no longer have access to the pastry kitchen, either."

"What is this, the Pentagon?"

Luciana ignores the sarcastic question. "You seem to enjoy spending most of your time here in Miss Glowin's pastry kitchen. I thought you'd be happiest there."

"I don't bake," Lena says through teeth grinding hard enough to raise sparks.

"Then this should be a stunning apprenticeship opportunity for you."

Lena takes two steps toward Luciana, close enough to feel the crimson leather of the woman's attaché case against her smock.

"Look, I know everything with a dick in this place has been treating you like the Sexy Pope, but that's no reason to exile the only woman on the goddamn line."

"Miss Tarr, this tone of yours—"

"Then fire me!" Lena shouts only inches from her face. "Oh wait, I forgot, I can't leave or the forces of Hell will hunt me down and tie me to a fucking stake!"

"Which is precisely why these increased security measures and streamlining are necessary," Luciana patiently explains.

Lena is practically shaking in frustration. She turns back toward the gate, through which she can see the rest of the line working on prep for the next Consoné event.

"Are you all enjoying this?" she shouts through the

bars. "Is this entertaining enough for you?"

Most of them don't even acknowledge her, including Dorsky, who is attending mechanically to breaking down crates of purple potatoes. He doesn't even seem to hear her.

Darren and James, at least, look up from their tasks. James seems particularly sympathetic. He smiles meekly and offers her a silent but animated "I'm sorry" with his lips.

Darren stares back at her openly, slightly wide-eyed. He spreads his arms out toward the rest of them as if to say, "I don't know what's going on either."

Lena turns back to Luciana. "Yeah, you're doing a bang-up job of keeping us safe. Has Boosha woken up from her coma yet?"

"The state in which that poor elderly woman kept that ramshackle work area of hers and the resulting accident are exactly the types of safety concerns I'm trying to address here."

"What are you *really* doing?" Lena demands of her.

Before Luciana can answer, Moon rounds the corner from the lobby and approaches the kitchen, oblivious to their presence. His attention is glued to the screen of the Nintendo 3DS in his hands. He almost impales himself on the wrought-iron barbs of the new barrier before he notices it.

"What the hell, man?" he squawks, finally taking notice of the two women. He reaches out and futilely yanks at the locked gate. "I want some of that leftover Henley's from the elementary gig."

"We threw that shit out," Lena snaps at him. "What's wrong with you?"

"Mr. Swarthout!" Luciana greets Moon, happily.

Lena silently mouths the name in shock, looking at Moon and momentarily forgetting her righteous anger.

"Would you mind guiding me to the Stocking & Receiving Department?" Luciana asks him. "I'd like to have a few words with you and your coworkers."

Moon blinks up at her, the usual giddy deference the men of Sin du Jour show Luciana absent from his face.

"Uh . . . yeah, I guess. I'm still hungry, though."

"I'm sure we can remedy that. Please . . ."

Luciana motions him up the corridor, and Moon slowly begins walking in that direction, eyeing the woman with a mixture of confusion and suspicion.

Lena watches them go off together, the wellspring of her rage bubbling anew. She goes bombing through the winding corridors and sudden staircases of the building that used to confuse and frustrate her, but now seem second nature. Sixty seconds later she finds the door to Bronko's office closed, but not locked. She turns the knob without knocking and flings open the door, storming into the room.

Bronko is reclining in the leather chair behind his desk, booted feet propped up on a purchase order on the desktop.

"What is this shit?" she demands. "You drag my ass back here and now you're banishing me from the line?"

Despite the brashness, Lena isn't out of control. In point of fact, on the short walk to his office she was consciously expecting, and even hoping for, the rain of verbal fire that will no doubt meet her show of abject defiance and lack of respect.

Instead, Bronko lolls to one side so he can wearily regard her sudden presence.

"I don't know what you're talkin' about, Tarr, and I am thoroughly uninterested in finding out."

His voice sounds like the creaking of a coffin, only with even less energy. Lena actually looks at him, really sees him for the first time since entering the room, and realizes she's seeing a man on the brink of exhaustive shutdown. The bags under Bronko's eyes could fit all the world's problems, and his expression says that's exactly what they're carrying.

"What's wrong with you?" she asks, suddenly losing the iron grip on that fiery rod of her anger. "Are you sleeping at all? Ever?

"I must be," Bronko muses. "I distinctly remember dreamin.'"

Lena finds herself at a loss. The preevolutionary reptile portion of her brain just wants to scream and fight and seek bloody satisfaction. The rational portion of her brain sees a beaten-down man she knows to be good, to care deeply for his people, and it sympathizes.

"Listen, Chef," she begins, more earnestly and with far less vitriol, "this Luciana chick—"

"Is the cost," Bronko finishes for her.

Lena just stares and blinks at him for several moments.

Bronko returns to staring at the wall. "Allensworth is all that's keeping this place bricked together. He knows it. He's using it as an excuse to put tighter reins on Sin du Jour. She's the reins."

"But, Chef—"

"Just do what she says, Tarr. What's the difference? You don't want to be here either way, right?"

That question cuts her more deeply than Lena would've thought after the way she returned to Sin du Jour.

"If I'm here, I'm here to cook," she says, her voice much quieter than it's been at any point in the last fifteen minutes.

Bronko looks back at her again, just for a moment, as if summing her up.

"Then you should decide if you're here or not. Shut the door on your way out."

It's obvious he'll have no more to say on the matter, or any matter. Lena stares at the side of his head defiantly for a while longer, but she knows the conversation is over, and whether it's true or not, she feels like she lost.

EXILE ON PASTRY STREET

Her third spumoni cupcake does nothing to salve Lena's rubbed-raw nerves.

She sits atop a stainless-steel counter behind Nikki in the small pastry kitchen wedged far into the east corner of the buildings where Lena's been exiled.

"So, really you're upset because she thinks you're a pastry puff," Nikki says, minding a pot of sugar and water she's bringing to a boil.

Lena frowns at her back. "I didn't say any stupid shit like that, did I? You know I respect what you do. It's just not what I do. Besides, you don't *need* me back here. You're the . . . whatever . . . Iggy Azalea of dessert."

Nikki looks at her, nose scrunched up in repulsion. "Um. Ew?"

"I don't know celebrities. Nik, she put a friggin' pair of gothic Dracula gates on the kitchen. Does that seem normal to you? Even for this place? And half the line is standing in there like robots. I yelled at Dorsky and he didn't even throw that shit-eating grin at me. I didn't even hear him make a dumbass joke about it."

Nikki, who had been stirring the contents of the near-boiling pot, stops. "That is weird, yeah."

"I know, right? It's more than just a corporate overlord cracking the whip. That chick is doing . . . something. I don't know."

As if on cue, Cindy's voice precedes her sudden entrance into the pastry kitchen: "Can y'all believe that cotdamned Becky Kardashian hipster bitch? I mean, really? *Really*?"

Lena and Nikki turn to see Cindy carrying a cardboard filing box, looking as aggravated as either of them have ever seen her, although they've rarely ever seen her visit the pastry kitchen.

"What happened?" Nikki asks.

Cindy slams the box down atop one of the prep stations and takes a deep breath, exhaling slowly.

"Italian CEO Barbie just shuttered Stocking & Receiving," she informs them both.

Nikki gasps. "Oh my god!"

Lena, on the other hand, just starts cursing.

"She said we don't need to be 'centralized on-site' or some such shit. She said we're a satellite operation, freelancers technically. Told us to pack up what crap we wanted to take from the hole and go home. We're to consider ourselves 'on-call.' I mean, she did give us new company Samsung Galaxys, but damn."

"Not to sound cold, but why are you telling us?" Lena asks. "We don't really . . . hang."

"That is *extremely* cold," Nikki chastises her.

"I mean, where are Ritter and the others!" Lena shouts back at her.

"No, she's right," Cindy says, seeming genuinely undisturbed. "We all got our own cliques. But that's the thing, though. Ever since this bitch came to town, the boys aren't the same. I mean, Moon is, but that's no damn help. Ritter and Hara didn't even give a shit when she axed our space just now. They just shrugged and packed up and left. No argument, no . . . nothing."

"I mean, they're not expressive guys—" Nikki begins.

"I am aware of that," Cindy snaps back at her, annoyed. "At first I thought it was just whatever shit happened between you two"—she nods at Lena—"which is none of my damn business, but Ritter isn't even feeling that anymore."

"Neither is Dorsky," Lena mutters more to herself than them.

Cindy's right eyebrow shoots up. "You fuckin' Dorsky, too?"

Lena narrows her eyes at her. "Stick with 'none of your damn business.'"

"Ladies," Nikki interjects, firmly. "Let's stay on target here."

"The 'target' is this *Growing Up Gotti* reject cousin ensnaring everything with a Y chromosome up in here and fucking with our world."

"It just doesn't make any sense," Lena reiterates. "She's supposed to be here to keep us safer, but all she's doing is dividing us. She got rid of Ryland. Your team. She kicked me out of the kitchen. She's been pushing Jett out of the picture since day one. And Boosha—"

Lena pauses then, thinking.

"What is it?" Nikki asks.

Lena eyes darken. She frowns.

"I don't believe in coincidence," she says. "I need to go. I'll be back."

Lena pushes herself off the counter and walks out of the kitchen without another word, or waiting for one from them.

Nikki watches her go, confused and troubled.

"That girl has a restlessness, you know?" Cindy observes.

"Yeah," is all Nikki offers on the subject. "Hey, you want a cupcake?"

Cindy looks at her, almost startled, for a moment. Then she slowly grins.

"Yes. Yes, I really would like a cupcake."

As Nikki retrieves a spumoni cupcake from a nearby freezer, Cindy looks at the box containing her few possessions from Stocking & Receiving's hole downstairs.

"What is up with Jett?" she asks Nikki. "I haven't seen a Chanel suit in days."

FAMOUS RED RAINCOAT

The horrifying and unspeakable truth is Jett hasn't worn a suit in well over a week. There's been no point. She hasn't been meeting with clients, the rest of the staff, or even Bronko. Her role at Sin du Jour has been reduced to almost nothing, and for no actionable cause by her reckoning. Chef Luck has never once expressed dissatisfaction with her work, as an event planner or coordinator, and a perfectly acceptable percentage aside neither have their clientele.

The only reason she even takes the E train to the office anymore is to feed her undead staff, the raised deceased who also haven't been contributing to Sin du Jour's events as of late. The saddest part is, Jett spends more time with them these days than anyone else in her life.

She strides purposefully through the corridors of the building, purse strap cradled in the crook of one arm while the other supports a pickle tub filled with fresh yak brains.

The door is a thick steel plate on sliding rails, covering a hole in the concrete wall. On the door, sloppily painted: "Alright Shamblers Lets Get Shamblin" (Moon did it, but Jett has long given up on wringing a confession from him).

Jett retrieves a large key from her weathered Coach bag only to find the lock it fits is open and dangling from the loose chain that usually tethers the slab to the wall. She frowns, returning the key to her bag. Tagging the door is one thing, but no one in the company is foolish enough to enter her employees' lounge without her, let alone leave it unlocked.

She grips the handle and inches it open, just a crack, testing. Nothing and no one attempts to leap out at her. Just to be safe, Jett digs into her bag and removes her Piece of the Dead, the small fleshy Bluetooth-like device that allows her to control her undead employees. Fitting it over one ear, Jett again grips the handle and yanks the door aside, walking into the room.

Two steps in she drops the pickle tub, splashing the leg of her running pants with yak's blood. Her purse strap slips from a suddenly slack arm, as well.

Luciana is standing in the middle of what's now a kill room, covered from head to toe in an elegant, translucent raincoat with pockets lined by thick white piping. The raincoat is splattered with viscous green and almost black red. In one gloved hand she cradles the haft of a large hatchet while the other grips the handle of a machete.

The blades of both tools are dripping with the same sickly juice and covered with matching gore.

Luciana turns and peers out from beneath the raincoat's clear hood at Jett, smiling calmly.

"Miss Hollinshead!"

Headless, decomposed bodies are strewn about the Astroturfed playroom Jett built to occupy the undead in their off hours, all of them still wearing their Sin du Jour work coveralls. Every single one of Jett's workers has been decapitated and permanently removed from the realm of the living.

Gary, a former sound engineer who died in a fire during a rock concert, is still clutching one of the room's large rubber balls in his gray hands.

"What have you done?" Jett demands.

"Oh, I've just completed a little spring cleaning. We decided your . . . employees . . . were simply too large a safety and security concern. And with your department being scaled back, they were also an unnecessary drain on resources."

"You had no right!" Jett shouts at her, furiously.

"No," Luciana corrects her, "*they* had no rights, Miss Hollinshead. Your staff relinquished them along with their grip on this mortal coil."

"That's not the point!" Another, equally horrifying thought strikes Jett. "What about Byron? Did he . . . was it . . . does he know about this?"

Luciana's smile doesn't change, but her eyes do, taking on something undeniably cold and almost gleeful.

"Of course," she says. "He is the boss, after all."

Jett begins walking toward her. "You bitch—"

She stops when Luciana raises her machete, holding it between them, its stained tip pointed at Jett's heart.

"Careful, little girl," Luciana says, and for the first time Jett can recall the woman has stopped smiling. "You're holding on to gainful employment by a very thin thread. I wouldn't go adding your personal safety to that already strained line."

Jett stares at the machete blade, then up at the face of the woman holding it. Jett isn't afraid, but as in all things, her mind concerns itself with realistically assessing the current situation.

She takes a step back.

Luciana slowly lowers the machete, and that smile returns to her face.

"Now, if you'll excuse me," she says, "I've got a cleaning crew coming in to sanitize the space. I think it'll make a fabulous converted stock room."

Jett swallows what feels like a dollop of hot lead.

"If you think I haven't survived worse than you," Jett says stonily, "then you've never planned a wedding for a reality television star."

With that, Jett kicks over the pickle tub dropped at her feet, spilling the inside of a dozen yaks' skulls all over the floor.

RELATIONSHIP MILESTONES

"Fuck!" Lena curses in frustration as she struggles to fit her key in the lock.

It occurs to her that rushing to unlock the door invariably leads to the process taking twice as long as it would've if she'd just operated at normal speed. Lena mentally tells that thought to go fuck itself too. She then curses herself for cursing her own thoughts, and by the time she's done with all of that she realizes she's still impotently and hurriedly stabbing the brass around the keyhole.

"Fuck!" she yells again, and finally manages to slide the key home.

Once inside, Lena unbuttons and pulls off her chef's smock, tossing it over the sofa. There are several of her tops on hooks she hung from the hallway lintel to dry after doing her laundry. Lena impatiently yanks one down and pulls it over the tank top she wears beneath her smock.

"Darren! Are you here?"

From his bedroom at the end of the hallway she hears

something that could be a muffled acknowledgment of her question.

Lena finds him neatly folding clothes on his bed and organizing them inside an open suitcase with an equally anally retentive attention to detail.

"Where the hell are you going?" she asks.

"Luciana gave me and James a few extra days off this weekend. We're going to take a trip upstate. There's this farmers' market in Rochester he's always wanted to go to."

Lena feels the subtle stabs of a headache coming on. "I . . . there are so many things you just said that I don't understand."

"What do you mean?"

"Why did she give you two, specifically, time off? Especially when we have Consoné's second speech coming up?"

Darren shrugs, continuing to pack.

"I dunno. I've been picking up a lot of slack while you were away. Now that you're back maybe she wanted to reward me."

"And James?"

"He works hard too."

"We all work hard."

"I mean, you do when you're here," Darren says without malice, but with definite reproach.

"All right, I'll take that hit. But I don't get how you can just, like, blow town with everything going on at Sin du Jour."

"Okay, again, you lecturing me on running out of town without telling anybody is kind of fucked up—"

"I've copped to it! Repeatedly! Can we move on?"

"All right. What's going on at Sin du Jour? Besides the usual stuff?"

Lena is practically gawking at him. "The usual stuff like all the forces of Hell wanting to kill us and fucking torment our souls eternally, you mean?"

"Yeah."

"Has that beard grown up through your jaw into your brain or something?"

"Leave me alone about the beard."

"Darren, for fuck sake, I like the tweaks you've made in my absence, but not being a little bitch doesn't mean being dense."

"I wasn't a little bitch."

"You were kind of a little bitch."

"I was kind of a little bitch, fine."

"She's taken over the damn company! Monrovio! How have you not noticed this? She locked me out of the fucking kitchen. Literally. She put a lock on the kitchen."

"Stuff goes wrong in the kitchen. Boosha and the Goblin wedding. That . . . the thing I accidentally let out that time. It probably should have a lock on it."

"And me being on the other side of that lock?"

"I don't know, dude, it's her and Bronko's call—"

"Her call."

"Either way. I don't know why she did it."

"Has it occurred to you at all that she seems to be systematically weeding out and isolating anything and anyone that doesn't want to fuck her?"

"Wow. You're not usually the catty girl type."

"You . . . what, are you saying I'm jealous of that bitch?"

"I didn't say."

"Fuck you."

Darren frowns. "What do you want me to do, Lena? Agree with you about everything all the time and not have an opinion? I'm through with that."

"Oh, what the fuck ever, man. Don't make me the boogeyman of this personal renaissance you're having or whatever it is. And don't act stupid because you want to go balls-deep in James in a bed-and-breakfast upstate. I'm watching the rest of the line work their stations like Jett's zombies. You saw it too. Something weird is happening, and it started happening when Monrovio showed up."

Darren shrugs again. "Have you thought about the idea that maybe it's not her. Maybe it's Dorsky. Like, maybe you being back and the way you left stuff with him is the reason he's not his usual self and the reason you're not on the line."

"And what about the others?"

"They take their cues from Dorsky, you know that."

"So, what? They're sympathy moping? Do you fucking hear yourself? The line, Bronko, practically the whole Stocking & Receiving crew, every hetero dude in our company looks and acts like they haven't slept in a week and somehow that's all my fault? I didn't fuck everybody, Darren, just two of them."

Darren's eyes widen. "Two? What?"

"What? One. Whatever. The point is, she's doing something and I want to know what, and why."

"Okay. Do what you do. I don't want to know any of that stuff, though."

"I'm going to visit Boosha in the hospital," Lena says, resolute. "All I want to know is are you going to be here when I get back?"

"No. I want a break. I need a break. You had one, a long one, and I want one too. With James. And I think you're overreacting to Luciana. She's just doing her job. I'm sorry that's pissing you off."

"I liked you better as a little bitch," Lena says, turning and striding out of the room.

"No, you didn't!" he shouts after her.

"No, I didn't!" she shouts back.

Darren nods to himself, satisfied. "See you on Monday!"

Out in the living room, he hears their front door slam shut.

VISITING HOURS

It's a special ward of Mount Sinai Hospital of Queens, one that receives very few human visitors because humans are never admitted there as patients.

"I've never seen anything like it," the doctor explains to Lena as he guides her through a hallway lined with unmarked doors. "And mind you, my job consists almost entirely of seeing things no one else has ever seen before."

He's human, it seems, the doctor is, with a deep baritone voice and a neat ponytail.

"The injuries she sustained in her accident were relatively minor, but they won't heal."

"Why not?"

"Boosha is a hybrid, seemingly of . . . well, everything. She has DNA from most known species we have on file, and DNA from species we haven't catalogued, and then there's some stuff that doesn't really qualify as DNA, but seems pretty important."

"Okay, but why would that stop her from healing herself?"

"Because it isn't all one thing, which makes almost no

sense. Actually, I'm wrong. It makes no sense. Boosha seems to be a collection of different genetic material existing independently of each other. When her body attempts to perform a simple operation, like healing a wound, that contrary material collides trying to perform the task and it all cancels each other out so nothing gets done."

Lena gives up trying to understand or even process that halfway through his explanation.

"So what are you going to *do*?" she asks.

"We're trying to figure out a way to neutralize her own internal processes and heal her ourselves. In the meantime, she's largely unresponsive. Hearing a familiar voice never hurts, though."

The doctor opens one of the unmarked doors and ushers Lena inside. Boosha's tucked into a small, plush bed in a simply appointed room. She's not hooked up to any machinery, not even a pulse monitor. Lena can see bruises on her cheek and forehead. Her skin is also tinted a sickly green, but Boosha's skin is always tinted a sickly green, so that's not particularly telling.

The doctor leaves them alone and Lena seats herself on the edge of the bed beside the comatose woman. She studies the features of Boosha's face, the eyes that are set just a little too far apart and shaped a little too octagonally to be entirely human.

"You know, you're about the furthest thing from normal I've ever met in my life, but you were actually the only one who made that place feel normal to me. Coming to you, listening to you tell us about all these things, all these creatures and their history, sounding like my Hungarian grandma, it made it all feel okay. You gave me some kind of anchor for things. I never once thanked you for that, and I should've."

Lena waits, unconsciously hoping for some reaction. When she receives none from Boosha, Lena realizes the futility of it all, speaking to her, Lena's suspicions, even coming here at all.

"You were telling me and Darren about the elementals," she presses on anyway. "Monrovio interrupted us. Boosha? You said you know what she is. What did you mean? Can you tell me? Somehow? Please? Everything's kind of gone tits up back . . . back home, even for that place, and I need to know what's happening."

Lena waits, and then waits some more.

The futility she was feeling a moment before becomes oppressive and undeniable.

Lena nods to herself. "That's okay," she says, softly. "Don't worry about it. You just rest, okay?"

She leans down and kisses Boosha's forehead, tasting copper and ash. The texture of her skin is like that of a palm leaf.

Lena stands up from the edge of the bed. She's turning to leave when Boosha shivers, visibly, under her gaze. Lena hesitates, watching her closely.

"Boosha?"

Her lips part, but there's no sound.

Lena slides back onto the bed and leans over her carefully. "What is it?"

Boosha's left hand twitches, then flops from the bed onto the bedside table. She taps one withered fingertip against the corner of the Gideon Bible lying there.

"The Bible?" Lena asks, confused.

The ancient woman shakes her head just so.

Lena's mind races. "Book?"

Boosha nods.

"Not this book, though."

Again, Boosha nods.

"One of your books? Back at Sin du Jour?"

Boosha's most emphatic nod yet.

BACKGROUND CHECK

"She's a goddamn succubus."

Nikki and Cindy stare blankly at Lena across the diner booth table.

It's obviously not the reaction Lena was expecting.

"Luciana Monrovio," she clarifies. "She's a succubus."

"Right," Cindy says, not disagreeing even a little.

"And?" Nikki asks.

Now it's Lena's turn to stare at them with her expression a void, at least until realization hits her.

"No! No, she's *actually* a succubus. Like, a real one. She's not human. She's a succubus and she's, like, magicked every Y chromosome in the company into being her mindless slave."

Lena reaches under the table on her side of the small booth they're sharing. She hefts a large tome with an intricately carved wooden cover protecting aging reams of papyrus. Dropping the volume down onto the table between them, she opens the book to a page she's marked with a receipt from the market attached to Kellogg's Diner, where she's convened this rare off-site meeting between the three.

Both pages are filled with one overwhelming illustration. Folds of inked-in black are wrapped around a mostly unseen figure but for a pair of narrowed feminine eyes peering above the top of the darkness. Piled beneath the curtained figure are men drawn as wrecked caricatures with Xs for eyes. Latin words, Japanese and Hebrew characters seem to be jammed together in those otherwise all-black panels.

"I'm pretty sure none of this says 'succubus,'" Cindy observes, examining the text.

"Yeah, turns out 'succubus' just means hooker in medieval Latin, which is . . . hypocritical and troubling in a wholly misogynistic way I can't deal with right now because we have bigger immediate issues."

"Granted," Nikki says.

"That is for real fucked up, though," Cindy adds.

"The entry in this book talks about Namaah, which is Jewish, and Kanjirottu Yakshi, which is Japanese, and I had to Google Translate and Wikipedia all this shit so I'm not pretending to be a demonologist, but the gist is they all correspond to a real thing, and 'succubus' is the most popular representation of that thing. It's a chick that holds men, or anything with a predilection toward women, in thrall by draining their free will."

"I mean . . . I feel that," Cindy says, "but how did you

go from one of Boosha's old-ass books to Monrovio being one?"

"Because Boosha left it for me. For us, I mean. That damn lectern of hers is the only thing still standing upright in her room, and this book was on it, turned to this page. She must've managed to put it there before she went out. I'm convinced Monrovio is the one who put her in that coma, too. Boosha knows what she is and Monrovio didn't want her telling anyone. She took Boosha out and made it look like Boosha's junkyard of an office finally collapsed on her."

Cindy taps her fingertips against the tabletop in rapid succession, several times, gaze removed in thought.

"Good enough for me," she proclaims a moment later. "Let's cut the bitch's head off and bury it behind a church."

Nikki frowns at her. "We're not killing anyone!"

"Any *thing*," Cindy corrects her.

"Nikki's right," Lena says. "We don't have enough information to take that kind of action. Yet."

Nikki frowns at her now too.

"So, what do you want to do, whistleblower?" Cindy asks.

"I want to get back inside the main kitchen, first of all. Monrovio went to a lot of trouble specifically to lock the women out of that place, and I'm almost positive that's why she's moving your department off-site, to get you out of the building, just in case. I want to know why."

"Breaking into a gate in our own building shouldn't be too tough," Cindy says.

"Should we get everyone else who Monrovio doesn't have her hooks in yet?" Nikki asks.

"Pretty sure you two are it at this point. Little Dove is off with that awful old man who calls himself her grandfather. Darren and James are getting sweaty upstate somewhere. I can't get a hold of Jett."

"There's someone we're forgetting," Cindy says, sounding dubious about even speaking the words.

"Who's that?" Lena asks.

ROOMIES

Darkness has mostly swallowed the row houses of Jamaica, Queens, by the time Lena and Cindy arrive at Moon's duplex.

"Only fair to warn you," Cindy says. "His place is a lot like a crack house without the folksy charm."

Lena almost grins. "Duly noted. But you're sure Monrovio doesn't have him?"

"I haven't run up against a spell yet didn't bounce off Moon like his ass is Scotchgarded."

They walk up the stairs to Moon's front door and Cindy pounds on it like an angry cop.

"Come in!" they hear Moon shout from inside the apartment.

Lena stares at her. "He leaves his fucking door unlocked?"

"I guess when you sustain your dwarfish ass solely on takeout and you don't want to stop playing video games, you'll risk the occasional murder."

Cindy turns the knob, opens the door, and ushers Lena inside graciously.

"Jesus, the smell," Lena mutters, hand over her mouth as she moves past Cindy.

They enter the exploded dumpster that is the front room to see a frenetic game of *Gears of War 4* being played on Moon's monstrous flat-screen television. Moon is seated on a sofa against the wall next to the door, controller held between his skinny legs. The coffee table in front of him is a landfill of fast food wrappers and stoner paraphernalia.

He's not alone, either. It's a two-player game raging on the screen, and the second player is wedged comfortably into the couch beside him.

It's Cupid, or at least the evil cherub version conjured in Hell and tasked with assassinating Satan's enemies on Earth.

Cupid apparently kicks ass at Xbox, too.

Suddenly the black Micarta handle of a dagger is in Cindy's hand; she moved so fast Lena didn't even see her draw it from the sheath concealed beneath her jacket.

"Get back!" Cindy yells.

"Will you calm down?" Moon snaps at her, annoyed. "He's my guest."

"Are you outta your cot-damned mind, boy? That thing's a demon assassin from Hell that was sent to kill your ass!"

"He's cool now," Moon assures her, sounding thoroughly casual about the whole thing. "We're off the hit list. And he didn't want to go back just yet. I guess they get all pissed off when you fail missions down there."

Beside him, Cupid nods emphatically.

"Moon," Cindy says, summoning every ounce of chill she possesses, "you're playing *Call of Duty* with a damn demon."

"It's the new *Gears of War*," he corrects her.

Again, Cupid nods.

"That ain't the point!" Cindy explodes.

"Look, I'm telling you, he's cool. Plus, I haven't had to pay rent for the past two months. Every time the landlord shows up, Q here shoots him in the ass with one of those depression arrows and the old man gets so sad he lets me off as long as I tell him he's a good person and people like him. It's fucked up, man."

This last Moon says with a chuckle.

"Oh hell, fuck it all," Cindy says, skinning back the lapel of her jacket and sliding the blade back into its sheath.

"Look, we need your help," Lena tells him.

"With what?" he asks distractedly, focusing on pulling off a headshot with his avatar's sniper rifle in the game. "And what are you two doin' hangin' out, anyway? Don't you both want to bone Ritter? I wouldn't think you'd be all *Sex and the City*."

"Wow, he really is an asshole," Lena says to Cindy.

Her eyes widen and Cindy spreads her arms helplessly. "Right?"

"So, what's up?" Moon asks, completely unperturbed by Lena's statement. "We were gonna order some Chinese or something."

As she's found is the best tack, Cindy is blunt with him: "We're breaking into Sin du Jour."

"Uh . . . you know we work there, right? They'll let us in."

"The kitchen," Lena clarifies. "That Monrovio bitch has locked all the women out of the kitchen. I want to know why."

"You know I'm not a girl or a cook, right?"

"I'm aware, but Cindy also said Monrovio doesn't seem to be able to get her hooks into you. She hasn't lulled you like the others."

Moon shrugs. "She's all right. Nice legs. I'm more into Asian chicks, though. Like, Southeast Asian, you know? Vietnamese and whatnot. Anime kinda killed Japanese chicks for me."

Cindy closes her eyes, shaking her head. "I hate . . . literally *everything* about what you are, Moon."

Moon laughs. "Yeah, I know. So why do I need to come?"

"I had an answer for that question," Lena says. "It's escaping me just now."

"Just get your ass off that couch and get in the car!" Cindy thunders at him. "You're part of the team. End of story."

Moon sighs, pausing the game with his controller.

"Fine." He looks at Cupid. "Don't finish the campaign without me, and lay off my fuckin' weed. My connect is doing thirty days in Riker's, so it has to last us."

Cupid nods at him.

Moon stands, digging through a pile of dirty clothes barricading the seat of a leather recliner next to the sofa. He eventually comes up with a wrinkled flannel shirt and begins laboriously pulling it over his slight frame.

Cindy and Lena watch him, Lena glancing around the front room while they wait.

"You ever think about hiring a maid, Moon?" she asks him.

He turns to blink at her, genuinely confused. "You mean, like, a hooker?"

Cindy raises an arm to stop Lena from pursuing the subject. "Just . . . don't. Don't, girl. Trust me."

Lena just nods.

MELLON

"How do we know Monrovio isn't skulking around here somewhere?" Nikki asks as they file through the darkened corridors of Sin du Jour hours past midnight.

Moon whispers back at her before fisting a bag of potato chips, "If you were gonna ask that question, why didn't you do it before we broke in?"

"We didn't break in," Lena hisses at him. "Two of us have keys."

"Will y'all please shut the hell up?" Cindy snaps at them. "It's like trying to infiltrate with three Moons instead of one."

Lena and Nikki both stop walking.

"Whoa now—"

"*Totally* uncalled for."

"I'm sorry," Cindy says immediately. "That was wrong."

Lena and Nikki look at each other, having a silent conversation with their eyes.

The two of them nod at Cindy, appeased.

They all start walking again, except for Moon.

"That was a slam, right?" he says. "Yeah, that was a

big slam. Fine. Whatever."

When they reach Sin du Jour's now gated and locked main kitchen, the space beyond the twisted wrought-iron bars is dark and empty.

Cindy unzips the small belt pack she's wearing, removing a few inches of clear plastic tubing filled with a dark compound.

"What is that?" Lena asks.

"It's just a little det cord filled with pentrite. It'll take out the lock without any fuss. Shouldn't even damage the rest of the door."

"How are we explaining the blown lock?" Nikki asks.

"We're chefs," Lena says. "We party. Shit gets blown up. It happens."

"That is true," Nikki says genuinely.

Shaking her head with a grin, Cindy feeds the thin line into the gate's lock. Removing a small aluminum cylinder, she backs up several steps and aims one end of it at the lock. Nothing much seems to happen, until it does.

Instead of burning, the cord in the lock explodes. It's little more than a few sparks and a "popping" sound that doesn't even cause an ear to ring, but it's more than enough to hollow out the cylinder of the lock.

"So cool!" Nikki whispers to Lena.

Cindy replaces the laser initiator back inside her belt

pack and zips it closed, stepping back up to the gate. She grips the handles on each barred door and turns each 180 degrees, flinging the gate open triumphantly.

At least, that's what's supposed to happen.

What actually happens is both gate handles seize as if they're still locked tight. Cindy tries to turn them again then jiggles them fiercely to no avail.

"Huh," is the best she can come up with.

Lena moves beside her and grips two of the bars. She gives Cindy a nod, and they both attempt to force the gate open, Lena pulling at the gate itself while Cindy tries to twist open the handles.

Nothing.

"Is it jammed?" Lena asks.

"There's nothing left to jam it," Cindy insists.

"Can I try?" Moon asks.

Cindy whirls on him. "What the hell you gonna try, Moon? Huh? Up, up, down, down, left, right, left, right, B, A?"

"I know you're makin' funna me, but I'm just impressed you know the Konami code. Now can I give it a shot or what?"

Cindy silently waves an arm at the seemingly indestructible door, stepping out of his way.

Moon digs out the final chip and pops it in his mouth, crumpling the plastic bag. He walks forward, holding out the balled-up snack wrapper to Cindy for her to take from him.

"Oh, fuck you," she says, folding her arms.

Moon shrugs, dropping it on the floor. He laces his fingers and cracks his knuckles, wiping both hands against his stained jeans. He hovers his hands over the handles of the gate, appearing to concentrate intently.

Watching him, Cindy rolls her eyes and begins muttering inaudible curses.

Ignoring her, Moon's hands inch slowly toward the gate handles. After an excruciatingly prolonged few more seconds he finally grips them tight and, with an expression of Herculean effort on his face, turns them until they click home and the two halves of the gate smoothly part.

Moon steps back from the now open gate, whistling casually.

The three women stare at him with open bewilderment, Cindy's tinged with open hostility.

" . . . how?"

It's an accusation as much as a question.

"It's enchanted," he explains. "The gate. No woman can open it."

"How do you know that?" Lena asks.

"I was in the pantry . . . totally *not* stealing anything, when that Monrovio chick brought the warlock in to do it."

"Why the hell didn't you say anything, Moon?" Cindy demands.

"You never ask me anything! All you do is order me around!"

"You are *not* my little brother—"

"The point is we're in!" Lena shouts over them, stepping between the two. "Can we just . . . ? Please? Okay?"

She ushers the rest of them through the now open gates and into the kitchen. The sea of stainless-steel prep stations are covered by trays containing an array of hors d'oeuvres, and layers of waxed paper and plastic cover those. Nikki peels at the edge of one to inspect the contents of the nearest tray.

"Looks like . . . rumaki? Sorta? Prosciutto-wrapped foie gras? On a stick?"

"Jesus," Lena says. "Is the theme of Consoné's speech 1970s culture that sucked?"

"What're we looking for?" Nikki asks.

"I don't know," Lena says. "But Monrovio wanted anyone she can't control out of here for a reason."

"And I doubt it was to make sure the menu was subpar," Cindy adds.

As the three women talk among themselves, Moon idly wanders between the grids of prep stations. He lifts one corner of the waxed paper covering dozens and dozens of hors d'oeuvres. Picking one up, he pops it in his mouth, chewing.

Lena sighs. "Maybe we're overthinking this. Just because she's a succubus doesn't mean she's got some evil plot going."

"This is an actual thing you just said right now?" Cindy asks, staring at her.

"I'm serious. We serve demons, goblins, centaurs, and . . . I don't even know what else. So she's a succubus. So what? She's a succubus trying to be an executive in New York City. She's using her . . . whatever . . . succubus-y powers to get ahead. Maybe locking us out of the kitchen is just a power move and nothing more. Maybe we're—"

The rest of Lena's defense of Luciana is interrupted by Moon, who abruptly lets out a shriek and drops to his knees on the kitchen floor, arms pressed into his stomach.

"You were saying?" Cindy says to Lena as they all crowd around him.

Nikki is hovering the closest, wracked with concern. "Moon? What's—"

"I'd stand back," Cindy warns her.

When Moon throws his head back and moans, he looks as though his face, neck, and arms have all turned purple. As he convulses, however, the three of them realize it's actually a thick purple substance being secreted from his every pore. He's sweating maroon, in buckets, and the uncontrollable gyration of his body sends the stuff flying in every direction, splattering Nikki in the face.

"Oh my god!" Nikki cries in disgust, wiping her face with her hands.

"Warned you," Cindy says.

"Is he dying?" Lena asks her.

Cindy shakes her head. "He doesn't do things that make my life easier."

Moon continues convulsing for the next twenty seconds. His clothes are thoroughly soaked through with the substance being expelled through his pores.

It ceases as quickly as it began.

"Man, that one sucked," Moon manages between panting breaths.

He rolls onto the floor and spreads out flat on his back, staring up at the ceiling with wide, glazed eyes.

"Moon, what the hell happened?" Lena asks.

"Oh. You know. Food's poisoned," he says, quite conversationally.

When the news sinks in, Lena's reaction is less horror than relief.

She looks at the others. "She poisoned all the food for the speech. Monrovio. She's put them all under some spell and had them spike the food. She's going to kill everybody at Consoné's next event."

Nikki is stunned. "Why would she want to do that?"

"Because she's a crazy evil cunt doing evil crazy cunt things!" Lena snaps. "I don't know!"

Meanwhile, Cindy is kneeling beside Moon with a kitchen towel, wiping away what's left of the discharge from his pores.

"Boy, you were either born entirely wrong or right in a way we won't ever understand," she says.

Cindy looks up at Lena and Nikki. "So what do we do?"

"Telling Chef Luck won't do any good," Nikki says. "He's just as turned around as the rest of them. Allensworth?"

"Allensworth's the one who sent her ass here," Cindy points out. "But why he'd be into a mess like this I can't figure out. It's supposed to be his job to keep everything on this side of the fence running smoothly. Assassinating a room full of goblin royalty and his own people? What does that get him?"

"I don't know," Lena says, "but Nikki's right. Going to him is out by default."

"Then what?" Cindy asks her.

Lena's expression becomes resolute. "We have to snap everybody out of it, especially Chef."

Nikki furrows her brows at her. "How, though?"

"Boosha's book said succubae don't ensnare men as much as they drain their will, make them complacent and docile so they can be controlled. They have to be aroused back to life, it said."

Nikki frowns. "I am *not* having sex with anyone on the line."

"Seconded," Cindy says.

"Are we including the two of you in this?" Moon asks.

"I'm not talking about that! It's, you know . . . adrenaline. Dopamine. We just have to get their stupid brains producing the right chemicals again. It'll break the spell long enough to get them back on our side, Bronko included."

They all fall silent, Nikki and Cindy both thinking to themselves intently.

Moon watches them. It's clear from his expression he is not thinking. About anything.

"Uh . . . are we supposed to be coming up with plans or something right now?" he asks.

"I got Ritter," Cindy says, ignoring him. "I know what to do. And after I get him we'll get Hara."

"*We'll* get them, you mean," Moon says. "I'm contributing here. I handled the door."

Nikki grins. "I know what to do about the line. I got this."

Lena nods. "Then that just leaves Bronko. For me. No

problem. No problem at all."

"How do we occupy Monrovio while all of this is going on?" Cindy asks.

"Luciana is mine," Jett insists.

They all turn to see her standing beneath the gated arch, watching them. Jett is wearing running pants and a tank top with an iPod strapped to her thin, steel-hard bicep. Her dark hair is bound in a severe ponytail and every inch of her exposed skin is flushed and glistening. She looks as if she's been out running for hours.

"Did you hear the rest?" Lena asks her.

Jett nods. "The rest of you just focus on getting our coworkers back. I'll take care of our new executive liaison."

Cindy grins at something she recognizes well in Jett's tone of voice. "How?"

"One of the most important rules of crisis communication in a corporate environment is to listen," Jett says. "That's what I'm going to do. I'm going to listen. To that bitch begging me for mercy."

PART III

LADIES' NIGHT

WHAT'S LOVE GOT TO
DO WITH IT?

All that's left of Stocking & Receiving is a fort made of packed boxes.

Cindy finds Ritter slumped over a folding card table in the otherwise barren space, staring sleepily at a small store-brand box of toothpicks. Many are the times she watched him build complex structures out of the cheap little splinters to test his manual dexterity and coordination after some injuries sustained on one of their gathering trips, either to his body or mind. It wasn't so long ago she'd watched him construct with his toothpicks after having his severed arm reattached on Lena and Darren's first day at Sin du Jour.

She walks past the miniature mountain range of flesh that is Hara, sprawled out on the floor near the boxes, not so much snoring as chewing invisible redwood trunks whole in his sleep.

Cindy stands in front of the card table, folding her arms and staring down at Ritter. "How you doing, droolly?"

He doesn't even look up. "Trying to summon the enthusiasm to haul these boxes out like Luciana told us to."

Cindy frowns at how much he doesn't sound like himself, in words, in tone, in spirit. She hopes Jett pummels Monrovio into a pair of bloody designer heels.

She takes a deep, steadying breath.

"I want to tell you a few things, shit I never had before, and now seems like a good time, what with you being all spell drunk."

His eyes roll up toward her just slightly. "I dunno what you're talking about, Cindy."

"I know. That's the point. That's why I'm going to tell you this shit now."

"Okay. Whatever."

"When you found me and offered me my spot on this team, you saved my life. If I had any doubts about that then, I sure as hell don't now. I wasn't lost, I knew exactly where I was going, and that was to my own damn grave, as fast as I could get there without just going and doing myself outright. I'll always love you for that, and for every day since.

"That's the other thing I want to tell you. Some days you're like my little brother and other days you're like my big brother, and I love you like that. I do. But you know that's not the only type of love I have for you. You give me all I need of the first kind, but I know you won't ever be able to return that other kind. And that's okay. That doesn't bother me none anymore. But me from years back always wanted to at least say it to you, and me now owed her that one. So I'm saying it."

"Okay," Ritter says, staring through her with his glazed eyes. "Are we done?"

"No," Cindy says, resolutely, and kicks him in the face.

It's not hard enough to break his bones, in fact Cindy took care to only send her leg out at half-speed, but the blow is more than enough to topple Ritter's chair and send him falling backward over it. He recovers slowly and awkwardly, wobbling on his feet when he finds them again. Both of his nostrils are rimmed with blood.

He looks at her like a blackout drunk who's just been ejected from the bar. "What . . . what . . . ?

Cindy reaches down and grips the edge of the card table, hurling it from her path as she strides toward him. Without another word she drives the heel of her right palm under his chin, snapping Ritter's head back. She hits him again the same way, this time aiming for the bridge of his nose, causing his eyes to cross and flash with phantom lights.

Ritter waves his arm, instinctually and lazily, trying to ward her off without really trying.

"Quit it, Cindy!"

"Well, that's a start," she says. "There's almost some bass in your voice."

Matt Wallace

Cindy twists at the waist to her left at an extreme an-
gle, allowing her to drive her right elbow powerfully into
Ritter's mouth and chin. He staggers back several steps,
cupping both hands over his face.

"Fuck!" he yells, and it's the most cognizant he's
sounded to her in days.

"There you go now! I know my boy's still in there
somewhere!"

Cindy advances on him, feet spread apart and fists
held aloft like a boxer. She begins peppering him with
sharp jabs, not throwing them hard enough to do serious
damage, but hard enough to get really annoying after the
first few.

Each blow seems to reshape Ritter's expression a little
more, turning the sallow, empty look he had when she
walked in the room into a bloody mask of anger and
eventually rage.

After the eighth jab, Cindy rears back and throws a big
right cross aimed at the center of Ritter's face.

His palm intercepts the blow, his fingers wrapping
around her fist and stopping it dead like a brick wall.

Cindy grins at him under their conjoined hands.

She's still grinning when Ritter's feet leave the ground,
his body pivots in midair, and he thrusts the sole of his
right foot into her chest.

Cindy loses the next several seconds to an inner abyss

and her next conscious thought occurs while she's sprawled out on the floor next to a still sleeping Hara.

Ritter is kneeling over her, his chest and shoulders heaving and blood dripping from several facial orifices both natural and unnatural.

"Jesus, Cin, I'm so sorry. Are you okay?"

"Of course I'm not okay, motherfucker! You titty-kicked me across the damn room! I should—"

Through the pain in her chest, back, and head, and the rage searing through her eyes, Cindy manages to really see Ritter for the first time since regaining her senses. What she sees pushes all other emotion and sensation into the background.

It's him. She's looking at Ritter, and Ritter, the real Ritter, is looking back at her.

"What the hell happened?" he asks her. "I feel like I just woke up from a nightmare I've been having for weeks, and why did I kick—"

"Succubus," Cindy says quickly. "Monrovio. She is one, I mean. She's had you in thrall for a goodly while now."

"Oh."

That information seems to put Ritter totally at ease, and his expression returns to its normal, unreadable state. He reaches out and offers her his arm, helping Cindy to her feet.

"That makes sense," he says. "Although the fact I didn't see it coming doesn't make me feel great about myself. Are you okay? Seriously?"

Cindy is holding both forearms against her breasts, breathing in and out slowly. "I owe you a good shot in the balls, but that'll keep for now. I'll be all right."

"So, what did I miss? And what did I do?"

"Later for that," Cindy says impatiently. "Right now, I need you to help me figure out how to snap Hara out of it, because I'm not punching him in the face, I'll tell you that right now."

Ritter peers down at the literal sleeping giant, thinking.

"Three or four syringes of adrenalin to the heart ought to do the trick."

Cindy raises an eyebrow at him. "For real?"

Ritter considers the question. "You're right. We'll make it five, just to be safe."

EXTREME INGREDIENTS

Nikki sits inside the darkened pantry of Sin du Jour's main kitchen, earbuds snugly tucked in and iPod piping a Richard Cheese album directly into her brain. The volume is low enough to be heard by her alone, and she's careful to mouth the lyrics to the stylish lounge covers of heavy metal and hip-hop songs silently. The line should be starting their shifts soon.

She's left the platter of brownies on an end table she brought in from home. It's placed strategically so it's the first thing in sight upon entering the kitchen. The brownies themselves she's stacked into a tall pyramid. Nikki has frosted each one brightly in green, purple, and gold, all of them dusted with a sparkling edible glitter; she wants the treats to be as eye-catching as possible.

The final touch is the note she placed in front of the brownie platter, addressed to the line, instructing them in simple, direct language to eat the entire platter.

Nikki signed the note with Luciana Monrovio's name.

She keeps the pantry door cracked so she can survey the scene in secret. Rollo, Chevet, and Tenryu shamble into the kitchen sometime after nine in the morning, dour, hollow-eyed, and single-file like workers in some Orwellian factory. Dorsky isn't with them, and Nikki hopes he's not far behind.

Rollo, the bear of a man looking even hairier and more unkempt now that he's lost what little free will he ever displayed as Dorsky's constant toadie, is the one to pick up and inspect the note. It takes him far longer to read the few lines than it should, and Nikki, still watching, wonders if that's a product of Luciana's influence, or if that would still be him on his best day.

Rollo silently passes the note among the other members of the line. The three of them obediently pick up a brownie and they each take a tired bite. In fact, their next several bites are mirror images of their first. Slowly, however, a new light infiltrates their eyes and they begin to eat with more vigor. By each of their third brownies they are practically jamming the confections whole into their mouths and swallowing without chewing.

In the pantry, Nikki has to restrain herself from clapping. Considering the sheer amount and variety of energy drinks she poured into that batter and had to mask with other flavors, it's less a victory and more a miracle they were able to choke down the brownies, let alone ingest enough to start frenzying on them.

Ten minutes later the platter is home to nothing but

crumbs and Chevet and Tenryu are running frantic laps throughout the grid of prep stations while Rollo dumps entire trays of poisoned rumaki into a commercial sink.

"Can you believe we cooked this shit?" he practically shrieks at the others. "What were we thinking? Are we a catering party for housewives in the fucking age of glasnost?"

Chevet and Tenryu laugh, grabbing the antiquated appetizers they prepared and throwing them at each other as they continue running like spastic five-year-olds around the kitchen.

Nikki can't believe how well her plan has worked. Not only did her baked Trojan horse snap them out of their fugue state, they're so horrified by the thoroughly uninspired food they prepared under Monrovio's control that they're destroying it, not even seeming to realize it's poison.

Nikki stands and begins an enthusiastic, albeit still silent, victory dance. She sways her hips, pointing at her own butt with both index fingers for no reason she'd be able to explain if someone were to ask her to verbally interpret the gesture.

Then she hears a familiar voice, albeit bereft of its usual verbal swagger: "What the hell did you guys do?"

It's Dorsky.

Nikki stops dancing and peers out through the crack

in the pantry door. He doesn't have the authoritative presence of a willful Dorsky, but he's still Bronko's sous-chef and second-in-command, and Rollo immediately stops purging their antique hors d'oeuvres.

"Boss," Rollo begins, still jacked from the spiked brownies and grinning like a madman, "I don't know, maybe we hit the bar too hard lately after work, but we cannot serve this splooge. It's beneath us."

Dorsky stares cow-eyed at him as if Rollo is from Mars.

"It's the menu Luciana gave us," he meekly insists. "You gotta stop—"

Without thinking, Nikki pulls open the pantry door and leaps back into the kitchen.

"Tag!" she shouts over him.

Dorsky's next word and the thought attached to it seems, thankfully, to die on the vine. He turns his attention from Rollo and the app massacre to regard her with a hangdog look of confusion.

"You're not supposed to be here," he says.

Nikki thinks about that for a moment. "Well then . . . you better come over here and make me leave, huh?"

It takes a while for Dorsky's succubus-addled brain to process the logic of that statement, but it obviously rings true to the orders he's been issued by Luciana.

Dorsky shuffles across the kitchen, the rest of the line

and the menu forgotten. As he draws near, Nikki backpedals slowly through the door, returning to the darkness of the large pantry. Dorsky follows her inside. Nikki manages to circle back around to the door once he's in the pantry, Dorsky almost tripping over his slowed feet as he attempts to stay with her erratic movements.

Nikki, still facing him, reaches behind herself and shuts the pantry door, jamming the lock with her earbud cord.

"What are you doing?" Dorsky finally asks.

Nikki stares at him in the darkness, the only light slicing through the cracks in the door from the kitchen beyond.

"Plan B, I guess," she says, taking a deep breath and letting it out slowly. "Okay. I'll definitely remind you again after, but . . . never, *ever* tell Lena about this."

Dorsky is still beginning to process the first few words of that statement when Nikki abruptly leaps at him, causing him to fall to the ground with her body smashed atop his. Any question or protest he might attempt is lost as she attacks his lips with her own, one of her surprisingly strong hands gripping him by the hair while the other hand delves beneath the waistband of his chef's pants.

Those who know Nikki well would have no problem likening her to a case of Red Bull in human form, even if they never imagined this particular application.

SLEEPLESS FOR HIS OWN REASONS

Lena stands outside the closed door to Bronko's office, staring at the deep lines of the mahogany wood. She's thinking about the times she's burst through this door without knocking over the past year. It seems to her now that every one of those occasions revolved around her burning desire to not work at Sin du Jour. She'd stormed Bronko's office, violating the most deep-seated of protocols regarding respect for one's executive chef, intent on not being pulled back into his world of monsters and magic and madness.

And every single time, Lena left Bronko's office to rejoin the line.

She knocks gently on the door. "Chef? Are you in there?"

"Perpetually," a ragged voice confirms from the other side.

Lena opens the door a foot and carefully peers around it, spotting Bronko's linebacker frame sunken into the cushions of a leather sofa wedged against the wall of his office.

"Sorry, Chef," she says. "Are you sleeping?"

"Those days are over, it seems. Come ahead if you're comin.'"

Lena slips inside. As she closes the door behind her, Bronko sits up with a deep groan. The noise he makes when he stands is barely human, except for the sound of half his bones popping. He shuffles around his desk and drops into the large wingback chair there.

Lena takes a seat across the desk from him in one of the simpler guest chairs.

He looks worse than he did before. The bags under his eyes are now more like gun turrets on a decaying B-52 bomber. He hasn't shaved in well over a week, and his skin has a sickly tinge to it.

"I'm sorry to bust in on you, Chef."

"That's never stopped you before. What do you need, Tarr?"

Instead of rising to that remark, or his question, Lena is quiet. She didn't tell Nikki or Cindy about this next part. She didn't share her thoughts or suspicions with either of them. At the time Lena assured herself it was because they'd protest or disagree, but the truth is she didn't tell them because she didn't know how to say it.

Now she has to say it to Bronko.

"I kept thinking about the last time I was in here, talking to you. I kept thinking about the look on your face and in your eyes, and how . . . it's not the same as every-one else around here lately. You're not quite the same as they are. And I don't think everyone would necessarily be able to see the difference, but I just happen to be unlucky enough to know that look. I saw it . . . I saw it over there, during my tour. I saw it on the faces of a lot of men and women. And I saw it in the mirror every day when I came back from Afghanistan. I saw it there for years."

Bronko sighs a deep, almost ancient-sounding weari-ness. "What're you plowin' at here, Tarr?"

Lena suddenly realizes she's not sure she can say it out loud, but in the end she also knows she's come too far to turn back.

She stares deep and probing into those raw, tortured eyes of his. "You know what Luciana is, don't you, Chef?"

"You mean a succubus?" Bronko replies flatly and without hesitation.

Lena falls against the seat back of her chair as if he's just jabbed her in the center of the chest with a pool cue.

"Yes," she says quietly. "A succubus."

Bronko nods. "Of course I know what she is. You don't think I know everything about my people?"

"So then . . . you're not under her spell or in her thrall or any of that."

"Of course not."

"Then . . . why do you look like this? Why are you acting this way? Why aren't you sleeping, Chef?"

For the first time in perhaps months, Lena sees Bronko smile. It's one of the top five saddest sights she's ever witnessed in the flesh.

"Tarr . . . you said you've seen what I've got goin' on here before." He waves one of his gnarled catcher's mitt hands around his face. "You say you saw it in the mirror. That's right?"

Lena nods.

"All right then, you tell me . . . what did you see back then when you closed your eyes?"

Of course, Lena can't answer him, and even if she had the ability to do so she would still probably refuse.

"Right," Bronko says. "Could you sleep?"

Lena shakes her head.

Bronko's smile only gains a new depth in its sadness.

"But . . ." Lena struggles, eyes searching his desktop as if she'll find her next sentence there. "Chef, why are you letting her do these things? Why did you let her take this place over?"

"What choice do I have, Tarr? Hell is nipping at the heels of all my kids here. Having that fire kiss my fat has-been ass is one thing, but I purely cannot abide it taking any of you. I won't abide that. And Allensworth is our only protection from it. There's nothin' and no one else in this world, prob- ably any other world. If his price is putting a few of y'all to sleep so he feels like he's in control—"

"What about Boosha, Chef?" Lena demands, leaning forward in her chair. "Monrovio almost killed her! Isn't Boosha one of us?"

For the first time, Bronko looks caught off guard. "Boosha . . . what . . . why would Luciana—"

"She had the line poison all the apps for Consoné's next speech! She's trying to use us to kill everyone in that audience! I don't know why, but it's true, Chef. I swear it. We have to stop her."

Bronko stares at her, seeing the urgency dripping from every contour of her face. He leans back into the deep leather folds of his chair, eyes darting from right to left as parts of his brain he'd practically shuttered kick back on and start spinning the rust off wheels.

"That son of a bitch," he says, and he might've forgotten Lena is even in the room. "That forked-tongued, snake-in-the-tall-grass, French-fried son of a bitch!"

Bronko bolts from the chair to his feet, and just seeing the silhouette of his former self is enough to spread a measure of relief throughout Lena's body.

He looks down at her, eyes burning. "Where's Luciana now?"

Lena meets his gaze, suddenly feeling like a high school kid in the principal's office. "Um . . . well . . . bear in mind this was part of a plan formulated when we all thought you were being held in the thrall of a sex demon—"

"Tarr!" Bronko warns.

"Jett," Lena says quickly. "Jett's . . . handling her."

FUCK SUN TZU

Luciana strides confidently through the lobby of Sin du Jour, the early afternoon sun pouring through the front windows at her back. She swings her vintage attaché case at her side while wearing the easy, unflappable smile half the staff has come to worship while the other half dreams of stripping it from her face with a fishhook.

That smile has yet to falter once during her tenure with the company, and it doesn't now even as Luciana finds her way is suddenly barred.

Jett is guarding the entrance to the main corridor like the Black Knight attending his bridge. She's clad in gym pants that cling to her legs and hips like a second skin, steel-toed Red Wing work boots, and a black athletic top. Her hair is coiled into a tight bun, and fingerless martial arts gloves cover her hands and knuckles.

"Did we join an intramural catering company cage fighting league of which I'm unaware?" Luciana asks her.

Jett grins. "Do you know what the best part of this is?"

Luciana moves her attaché case in front of her body, grasping its handle with both hands. In answer to Jett's question, she shakes her head pleasantly.

"I don't have to listen to any more of your bullshit," Jett says, deftly fitting a plastic mouth guard over her upper teeth.

Luciana actually laughs. "Very well then, Miss Hollinshead. I suppose this was inevitable."

One of her hands moves to unsnap the left latch on her attaché case. Unfortunately for Luciana her fingers never touch polished brass. She hasn't finished her last sentence when Jett unleashes a war cry worthy of an ancient Celtic army and leaps at her, driving a flying knee into Luciana's sternum. She goes down and the attaché case goes flying from her hand, landing near the front doors.

When Luciana stands up to face her again, Jett slams a right cross into her jaw. It finally wipes the smile from Luciana's face.

"That's for my staff!"

She follows it with a left to the cheek.

"*That's* for coming between me and Byron!"

Jett launches an uppercut that tilts Luciana's head enough for the hall lights to blind her.

"And that's for trying to show up my wardrobe, you *obvious* outlet whore!"

Jett grabs two handfuls of the shoulder pads in Luciana's suit jacket. The woman-who-isn't-really-a-woman's eyes are as glazed over as the men she wraps up in her will-draining web.

"And last but not least, *this* is for trying to take away my home."

Jett drives the top of her forehead into Luciana's mouth and chin with shocking power. The blow knocks her out of her thousand-dollar pumps and flat onto her back. Luciana achingly rolls onto her stomach, spitting blood and teeth at the lobby floor.

Jett pulls out her mouth guard, flicking it at Luciana's prone back.

"Should have ... ripped your eyes out ... on my first day," Luciana growls through the gaps in her clenched teeth.

"And just how would you have gone about accomplishing that?" Jett asks.

Luciana is already crawling forward, and Jett is more than happy to stand back and let her slink back out through the door and away from Sin du Jour forever.

It's not the door she's seeking, however.

Luciana reaches out and grips the edges of her discarded attaché case. In answer to Jett's question, she flips open both latches simultaneously.

As soon as the lid of the case is cracked, ethereal streamers of pure black begin shooting from every side. Luciana rolls onto her back, grinning up at Jett with her suddenly horrific maw. The black tendrils begin enveloping her, encircling her every limb like kudzu. In the next moment they're lifting her body off the lobby floor, raising her to an elevated position several feet above Jett's head.

Jett raises her fists reflexively, but she's already backpedaling, at a loss as to what's happening in front of her. The tendrils become rolling curtains of pitch darkness that shimmer about Luciana before enveloping her utterly. That darkness becomes a tornado, churning and twisting until it has stripped away Luciana's human form. In its place, rising above the mouth of the funnel, is the emaciated face and hairless skull of an albino demon with eyes made of black flame.

A tendril shoots out from the body of the darkness, slamming Jett in the chest and pushing her back to the lobby floor. The living shadow hovers menacingly above her, Luciana's eyes burning within its depths like the hearts of twin suns.

"The old woman was just a nuisance that required a minor adjustment," an inhumanly deep voice speaks to her from the heart of the void. "But you . . . I'm going to lick the flesh from your bones with a thousand tongues made of dark fire."

"Yes, well, I still knocked your fucking veneers out," Jett spits back at her, although her voice is shaking fiercely.

Jett tells herself she's ready, and that she won't give the

hellion bitch the satisfaction of hearing her scream.

She almost believes it, too.

The tip of a blade pierces through the center of the black maelstrom above Jett. Luciana's demon visage screams horribly. Around the protruding end of the double-sided blade, the rippling darkness suddenly recedes, streaming back across the lobby and into the recesses of the attaché case from which it emerged.

What's left in the wake of that darkness is Luciana's human form, with her battered and bloody face and rumpled suit, the blade sticking out of her left shoulder. A towering, bearded man in a dark suit stands behind her, holding the unseen haft of the dagger. When he pulls the blade from her body cavity, Luciana collapses onto her hands and knees in front of Jett. She begins frantically and agonizingly crawling away from her attacker, ignoring Jett's prone form entirely as she skitters past.

The knife-wielding man advances on them both, his face a mask of indifference, save for eyes that contain all the dark determination of an assassin.

Jett begins shaking her head as he points those eyes, and the tip of his blade, at her.

"Wait," she begins to say, but stops as he raises the dagger above his head.

Jett shuts her eyes tight and buries her chin against her chest, waiting for whatever comes next.

As it turns out, what comes next is the cavalry.

When the strike she's bracing against fails to descend, Jett opens her eyes and sees Hara restraining the man in his massive arms, hugging him into utter submission. The towering assassin looks like nothing more than a fussy baby refusing to suckle at the giant's breast.

The rest of the staff is pouring into the lobby. The next thing Jett knows, Bronko is leaning over her, reaching out to gently take her wrists and pull her up to her feet. He embraces Jett warmly with both arms.

"I'm so sorry, girl," he whispers into her hair.

Jett buries her face gratefully into his chest and focuses on holding back her tears.

"It's not your fault, Byron," she assures him.

"Hey, I recognize this guy," Lena says, examining the face of the man Hara is restraining. "He's Consoné's bodyguard."

"He tried to kill Luciana!" Jett informs them all. "He kinda-sorta saved my life, but I think that was accidental."

Cindy and Ritter are detaining a wounded Luciana several yards inside the main corridor. She begins shrieking, enraged, not at any of them, but at the man who ran her through with the dagger.

His voice, a deep baritone, booms back at her in the same language, one that none of them have ever heard before, not even Hara, who has mastered more dialects than a symposium of linguistic professors combined.

"Both of you shut the hell up!" Bronko thunders over the two. "Now!"

The mystery language shouting match ceases.

"Take Mongo there to Stocking & Receiving and hog-tie him with some heavy-ass chains," Bronko orders. "Then take our *former* executive liaison to my office and someone get a first aid kit and see to her wounds. We'll figure this thing out from there."

Ritter, Cindy, and Hara haul their new captives away to their separate makeshift cells.

"Tag!" Bronko calls out, searching the lobby for him.

Dorsky pushes his way through the rest of the line, straightening his chef's smock and clearing his throat.

"Yeah, Chef."

Bronko pauses. Something about his sous-chef's manner raises an alarm in his head, but he shakes the thought away.

"Go get a torch," he instructs Dorsky. "Turn that god-damn hipster briefcase of Monrovio's into bacon."

Dorsky nods. "Will do, Chef."

He turns too quickly and collides with Nikki, who stiffens like she's been hit with a cattle prod. Dorsky's re-action is a mirror image. They both make awkward, in-audible sounds of contrition as Dorsky quickly moves past her.

"Are you blushing?" Lena asks her a moment later.

Nikki suddenly can't stop blinking. "What? No. Shut up. No."

PAN-FRIED

In the industrial hole Stocking & Receiving once again calls home, Cindy and Moon are unpacking boxes while Ritter places a chair in front of the one to which they've bound Enzo Consoné's bodyguard. Hara is looming close to the stoic assassin, watching him intently.

Ritter straddles his chair backward. He's holding the dagger used to maim Luciana and threaten Jett. Its handle is carved shale the color of sun-baked mud. The tip of the blade is pronged like a fishing spear. Ritter turns it over and over in his hands, examining it.

"This is a Venus dagger, isn't it? I've never seen one up close before."

The dagger's owner remains silent.

Lena and Nikki follow Bronko into Stocking & Receiving.

"He talkin'?" Bronko asks Ritter, who shakes his head.

Bronko addresses their prisoner directly: "How about it, son? Even a good soldier gives up their name, rank, and serial number. I'll settle for just a name. It ain't like we don't know who you work for."

The man looks up at Bronko, his expression unchanging. He does, however, maintain eye contact for a good ten seconds.

"Claudius," he finally says, his voice deep and surprisingly quiet.

Bronko nods. "Claudius. Good. Well, I'll go ahead and assume you know me. You came here with a succubus-killin' knife to kill a succubus. That succubus was plottin' to murder damn near everybody at your boss's next fireside chat. That seems clear enough. What's confusin' me is what the beef is between y'all. I was hoping you could enlighten me on that score."

Claudius returns to staring at the wall.

Bronko sighs. "Listen, son, I don't feel the need to convey to you how serious this business here is. You know that. What you need to know is I don't give a tinker's damn about politics, what I care about is my people and us being caught in the middle—"

Bronko stops talking. He's watching Hara, quite out of character in Bronko's admittedly limited experience of the man, lean down and whisper something inaudibly to Ritter.

"No shit," Ritter says out loud, though there's little to no inflection on the words.

"What's up?" Bronko asks him.

Ritter stands, sweeping the chair out of his way. He flips the dagger in his hand, thoughtfully.

"My big man here," he says, pointing the blade at Hara, "noticed something . . . let's say enlightening, while he was hugging on our guest back in the lobby."

Lena and Nikki trade questioning glances while Bronko tilts his head, grinning.

"And what might that be, Mr. Thane?"

Ritter takes two steps toward Claudius, who doesn't even acknowledge Ritter's presence. Ritter holds up the dagger's blade in front of the man's face, then deftly reverses his grip on the knife, slashing the blade down through the left leg of Claudius's suit pants. He repeats the slice on the right leg, reaching out with his free hand and gripping the material, tearing the man's pants away entirely and flinging them across the room.

"What the *fuck* is that?" Lena blurts out, immediately covering her mouth with her hand.

"Is that real?" Nikki asks.

Claudius doesn't have human legs; he has the shaggy hind legs of a goat. His dress shoes are affixed to two giant cloven hooves by a series of straps.

"He's a Satyr," Ritter explains.

Claudius' expression hasn't changed, but he does swallow hard under the scrutiny.

Bronko watches him, frowning. "Well, now I feel like an ass. Throw a blanket over him, will ya? Give the boy his dignity."

Hara retrieves a reflective emergency blanket from one of their open boxes and covers Claudius's lap with it.

"So, what does this mean?" Lena asks.

"Satyrs are the only race one hundred percent immune to the influence of a succubus," Bronko explains.

"Good choice for an assassin, then," Nikki says.

"But what does this *mean*?" Lena asks again.

Bronko looks at Ritter, who turns to address Lena and Nikki.

"In these modern times of ours," he says, "Satyrs are often gainfully employed by one race with a very specific interest in protecting themselves against the influence of succubae."

Lena waits, becoming annoyed with the fact that she's waiting pretty damn quick.

"Will you spit it out and knock off the murder-mystery weekend crap already—oh wait, you're doing this on purpose, aren't you? This is revenge?"

Ritter doesn't quite grin, but he does shrug.

"Revenge for what?" he asks.

Lena just narrows her eyes at him.

"Ritt," Bronko half-chastises him. "Just tell 'em."

Lena's groan is almost a growl.

"Jesus! Tell us *what*?"

THE CANDIDATE

"You're not human," Lena tells Enzo Consoné.

His suite at the Four Seasons Hotel is larger than any home in which Lena has ever lived, with a view of Central Park (and pretty much the entire city surrounding it) that must cost upwards of thirty thousand dollars a night. He's received them in a quaint sitting area with plush sofas and a glass coffee table between them.

"I was gonna open with something akin to, 'Thanks for seeing us,'" Bronko says to him, "but Chef Tarr here is more direct."

"That's quite all right," Consoné says with a winning smile.

Unlike Luciana, he manages it without seeming patronizing or artificial.

Consoné leans forward and pours the three of them a half-flute of champagne. He tops them off with a splash of fresh orange juice from a carafe next to the ice bucket.

"I appreciate directness. I try to cut through the bullshit myself. Not easy when you're running for public office, particularly a public that's more private than any private society on the planet."

"You're an incubus," Lena says, ignoring his palaver, as charming as she might find it. "You're the male version of a succubus."

"I am, yes," Consoné confirms without hesitation. "Please, enjoy a mimosa with me."

"Don't hafta ask me twice," Bronko says, picking up one of the flutes and tapping it against Consoné's as he does the same.

Bronko has drained his mimosa before Lena has time to seriously contemplate hers. She watches him do it with a gaping expression on her face, wanting to tell him he's totally undercutting her thunder here.

"Anyway," Lena says. "We do have a situation to discuss here, Chef."

"Right. So, y'all are both 'buses with a passion for Italian skins," Bronko observes. "You and Luciana Monrovio, that is. And I'd ask you if you know her, but since you tried to have her killed it's a safe bet you do. That all seems one helluva coincidence to me, Mr. Consoné."

"Luciana is my sister," he says. "I'm afraid we don't get along. We had a parting of the ways some time ago. Or rather, the man you know as Allensworth and I had a parting of the ways some time ago. Luciana, unfortunately, chose to side with him and his . . . organization."

Bronko frowns deeply. "Well then . . . that's pretty

much exactly what I did not want to hear."

"I'm very sorry," Consoné says, and he actually sounds sincere. "I'm sorry you were caught up in this. You seemed a convenient weapon to them, and so you were."

"What were they trying to do?" Lena asks. "Kill you?"

"No. From what you've said, they wanted my speech to the goblin hierarchy and the human contingent to go disastrously awry. If everyone but me were killed at such an event, the suspicion it would cast on me would be insurmountable for my campaign, possibly even my freedom, or life."

"You knew they were going to try something," Lena says, and it's not a question.

Consoné nods. "Though I couldn't predict precisely what."

"When I watched your speech, my friends were ready to throw their underwear at your head. You didn't have any effect on me. Am I special, or did you do that?"

"Can't both be true?" Consoné asks with a wicked grin.

Lena glowers at him.

Consoné laughs. "I'm sorry. Bad habit. I'm good at reading people, Chef Tarr. I read you as a fighter, a leader, someone fiercely protective of her comrades and compatriots who would root and cast out an influence like Luciana threatening them. So I . . . nudged you."

"I'm sorry it didn't work."

"Oh, it worked. It just . . . took a little too long. We were coming down to the wire. I'm not immune to panic. I apologize for Claudius. I apologize for sending him into your place of business, and for threatening your staff. This was not my intention. But I simply could not allow Luciana to carry out whatever machinations she and Allensworth were preparing."

"Why does he want you out?" Bronko asks. "Why does he care who becomes president of the *Sceadu*?"

"Your Allensworth . . . he's far more than he presents himself to you. This Henry Kissinger of the extrahuman world performance of his is just that. He has his own designs, his own ambitions, and I don't fit into them. I'm not a puppet. I have my own ideas for the future of my race and the other forgotten races of this world."

Bronko stares into his empty champagne flute, processing that. His expression becomes so heavy with concern Lena finds herself watching him, worried.

Eventually he looks up at Consoné.

"Is there a war coming?" he asks the candidate.

Consoné smiles at him, a sad smile very much like the one Lena found Bronko leveling at her back in his office.

"Chef Luck," he says, "the war started quite a while ago. But . . . you just cook the food. What have you to fear?"

Bronko nods, his expression unchanged. "Right. Well. Thank you for your time. I believe you've answered all of our questions as generously as can be expected of you."

They all stand, as if on cue.

"It was my pleasure, Chef. I'm a big fan of yours. And your fare for my events here has been flawless. Thank you for that. And again, I apologize for the position this all wedged you into."

"Oh, I almost forgot," Bronko says, reaching inside his smock and placing Claudius's Venus dagger on the table between them.

He takes out his wallet and removes a hundred-dollar bill, folding it in half and balancing it atop the flat of the blade.

"So your man can buy himself a new pair of pants," he says. "That was our bad."

"Thank you, Chef. I respect an individual with a sense of their own personal debt."

"I know what I owe, Mr. Consoné," Bronko says, darkly. "I know what I owe."

He carefully navigates the space between the sofas and the delicate-looking glass furniture.

Lena finds herself lingering behind, gaze held by Consoné's.

"Is there something else with which I can assist you, Chef Tarr?"

"You were some kind of guru, right? Before you ran for . . . whatever. You advised people. Powerful people."

"I always offer counsel to my friends, when it's requested. Do you have a problem?"

"A couple of 'em, actually. I . . ." Lena hesitates. "You know what? Nevermind. Thanks for being honest with us."

"If you change your mind, I expect we'll run across each other again. There'll be a wealth of catered events in my immediate future."

"Right. Good luck in the election."

"Thank you."

Lena is suddenly in a great hurry to escape Enzo Consoné's line of sight.

"So, what are we going to do, Chef?" Lena asks Bronko when they're alone in the hotel elevator.

"We'll hand Luciana over to Allensworth. No other choice, really. We'll gamble he's more pissed about her failing than us monkey wrenchin' another one of his schemes. We'll gamble he's got bigger concerns than us just now. We'll gamble and we'll lose, because that motherfucker knows everything. But there's nothing else we can do."

"Then what's going to happen?"

Bronko shrugs. "Folks still gotta eat, Tarr. I expect he'll get over it."

Lena looks up at him, suddenly feeling more lost and afraid than she's allowed herself to feel in years.

"What if he doesn't?" she asks. "What if he doesn't get over it?"

Bronko sighs. He rests a hand gently on her, practically encompassing her shoulder in his grip.

"We'll try to be ready," he says. "And if Hell's comin' for us, then Hell is what we'll give 'em."

EPILOGUE
MISSING FROM YOUR TO-DO LIST

Ritter feels as though he hasn't been home in a month, and even if that's not true, a large part of him hasn't been leaving the office lately. He'll be surprised if his brother isn't renting the place out, or hasn't turned it into a flophouse, or both by now.

The first thing Ritter hears as he opens his front door is Stravinsky playing over his absurdly expensive sound system. This is particularly odd, as the only classical music his brother has ever listened to is REO Speedwagon.

"Marcus!" he calls out, receiving no answer.

Frowning, Ritter retrieves his dragon bone–loaded shotgun from the coat closet and ascends the steps to the first level of his home, holding the weapon at the ready.

The first thing he sees over the shotgun's sights is Allensworth, sitting at Ritter's dining room table with his feet propped up next to an open box with a half-eaten pizza inside it. He's holding a slice, waving it like a maestro's wand to the music.

"Ritter!" Allensworth greets him. "Welcome home!

Your brother ordered pizza. It's delicious. You have some *lovely* eateries in this neighborhood."

Ritter lowers the shotgun, though he doesn't relinquish his grip on it. He knows it would be a last-ditch effort, however. Allensworth is always prepared, and for the absolute worst.

Marcus is kneeling, naked, on the carpet. His wrists have been duct-taped behind his back. His ankles have also been taped together, and blood from his nose has run over the strip covering his mouth. He stares up at Ritter with desperate, pleading eyes.

A rotund man wearing a dark Armani suit and an executioner's hood is holding the muzzle of a suppressed automatic pistol to the back of Marcus's head.

Allensworth replaces the slice of pizza in its box and wipes his hands against each other.

"It seems your brother lost his way en route to his team's next mission," he observes, sounding thoroughly neutral in the matter. "Which is a shame. They're having a bear of a year with ice harpies in the Alaskan Range."

"This is just a misunderstanding," Ritter assures him.

Allensworth nods. "I see. How have I misunderstood you harboring a deserter, exactly? Your brother or no, that's just bad form, Ritter. Especially with the favor I've shown you in the past."

Ritter keeps his voice calm and even. "I meant to call

you. We've all been very . . . distracted at the office lately. I'm afraid it fell by the wayside."

"Ah, yes. I see. Well . . . your timing always was abysmal, I'm afraid."

Ritter can feel the pulse in his fingertip beating against the trigger of the shotgun. If he goes for it, is Marcus cognizant enough to hit the deck as soon as Ritter begins raising the weapon? If he doesn't, the blast will never reach the executioner before he squeezes his own trigger and puts a bullet through Marcus's brain.

"Now, Ritter," Allensworth begins, with a sudden gravitas, "you have several options at this point. Would you like me to tell you about the ones that don't involve a shootout?"

Ritter stares into his brother's terrified eyes, holding his gaze like a lifeline. His mind is playing out every permutation of what's to follow.

Several dozen mental bloodbaths later, he bends at the knees and carefully places his shotgun on the carpet.

"All right," he says to Allensworth. "Let's talk options."

About the Author

Photograph by Earl Newton

MATT WALLACE is the author of *The Next Fix, The Failed Cities,* and his other novella series, Slingers. He's also penned more than one hundred short stories, a few of which have won awards and been nominated for others, in addition to writing for film and television. In his youth he traveled the world as a professional wrestler and un-armed combat and self-defense instructor before retiring to write full-time.

He now resides in Los Angeles with the love of his life and inspiration for Sin du Jour's resident pastry chef.

TOR·COM

Science fiction. Fantasy. The universe.

And related subjects.

*

More than just a publisher's website, *Tor.com*

is a venue for **original fiction, comics,** and

discussion of the entire field of SF and fantasy,

in all media and from all sources. Visit our site

today—and join the conversation yourself.